'Meg, this is Jonathan Drew.'

'Actually,' she said in a shaken voice, 'we've already met. But it was a long time ago,' she added hastily, in case he didn't remember her.

But he did.

'Small world,' he remarked earnestly.

She nodded seriously. 'Long time no see,' she responded with due solemnity. The cliché game, which they'd played together in their irreverent youth. Her mouth quirked, and she grinned delightedly. At that moment, all her problems were forgotten.

Dear Reader

We don't travel far this month, but there is compensation in welcoming back Elizabeth Harrison after a long absence — also Stella Whitelaw and Janet Ferguson. The warmth they generate between their characters is lovely, and I'm sure you'll find their romances fascinating. We also have Caroline Anderson back again after the mammoth work she put into her trilogy, moving out of the hospital setting to explore the problems encountered by a working mother in general practice. Lots of pleasurable reading!

The Editor

After several years as a medical secretary in London hospitals and in general practice, **Elizabeth Harrison** went to a voluntary medical organisation as Associate Editor. Here she was responsible for arranging programmes in the U.K. for postgraduate doctors and nurses from overseas. She enjoys pottering about in boats, cooking in a slapdash way and trying to keep up with her garden overlooking Richmond Park. She is Vice-President of the Romantic Novelists' Association.

Recent titles by the same author:

THE SURGEON SHE MARRIED
A SURGEON AT ST MARK'S

CHAPTER ONE

NO WAY was she going to have one of those stupid crying sessions now, sitting out here in the car park. She couldn't be so feeble. Rupert wasn't that important. Only a good-looking surgeon with whom she'd had a brief affair.

A dear man she'd loved, and who had, for a few short, brilliant months, loved her.

That time was over. Come on, Meg Ashton, climb out of this car and go on in. You can handle it.

From the outset she'd been warned. 'You do realise he isn't serious?' anxious friends had regularly enquired. 'I mean,' they'd pointed out firmly, 'it isn't going to last, you do see that? With Rupert it never does.'

'Of course it doesn't,' she had assured them with a casual confidence she had inwardly recognised as phoney. 'We all know Rupert. Great fun to go around with, though, and I'm going to have a bit of the action while it's on offer. I'd be mad not to, wouldn't you say?'

'As long as you understand,' they'd responded uneasily.

'I understand absolutely,' she had maintained cheerfully. At first it had been true. 'I'm one of a series, that's all—a fairly long series. Rupert's latest.'

That had indeed been all. And now she no longer

had the faintest idea how to manage without him. Somehow, though, she'd got to. So get out of this car, Sister Ashton, she told herself, and put one foot in front of the other until you're back in your own ward.

Reluctantly she embarked on this trek, treading purposefully along to the cloakrooms, changing into uniform, hanging her anorak, jeans and sweater in her locker. For months, in case Rupert had wanted her to go out in the evening, she hadn't risked arriving in jeans. Throughout that magical summer, too, she'd spent wildly on her wardrobe, choosing outfits that were not only hideously expensive but, compared to the gear she'd worn during the rest of her twenty-six years, incredibly chic — even dramatic.

She had come full circle. Here she was in jeans and trainers and her anorak. Her new and enchantingly cut anorak, though, which until her eye had been trained by that rat Rupert she would never have picked out. She checked in the mirror. She looked a bit pale, but then she usually did. And her skin was clear, her hair gleaming. She was, after all, perfectly healthy. She didn't look a muddy green, haggard and ill, even if that was exactly how she felt.

Head high, shoulders back, a tall, slim girl in sister's blue with the flyaway cap they still wore at St Mark's perched jauntily on her short dark hair, she sailed along the corridor towards the orthopaedic block. Into battle, and all flags flying, she told herself, perhaps a little desperately, as she saw Duncan Baird, senior orthopaedic registrar, approaching. What she never suspected was that she was surrounded by hordes of rather angry well-wishers. Half the hospital was ranged up loyally behind her. Since her departure alone for the holiday they all knew she had expected to share with Rupert, he had been effectively sent to Coventry. A strong contingent of Meg Ashton supporters vowed to avenge — well, what, for Pete's sake? Hardly her honour, surely? In this day and age?

'Hi, Meg,' Duncan greeted her cautiously. 'How are you?' His glance assessed her.

'Great, thanks.' Determined to show herself cool, unflustered, she flinched inwardly as his eye scanned her. This was what she had to expect; she'd known that. Kind words and probing looks. That there might be sympathy and concern behind the scrutiny didn't cross her mind, and even if it had it would have upset her. The last thing she wanted was for anyone to guess how awful she felt. 'How have things been here?' she asked.

'Oh, not so bad. But Barbara isn't you. The list seemed to take forever to organise, and made us realise how fantastically efficient — not to mention fast — you are. We've all missed you.'

'That's nice,' she told him, with that sudden smile that so transformed her, had she only guessed it. But, unusually, she didn't dare meet his eyes. He'd be sure to read more than she intended him to see. 'Nothing like a little appreciation,' she added lightly, looking past him along the corridor. 'I go for that.'

'Don't we all?' he agreed, equally lightly, though his eyes remained searching. 'See you later — in the side-ward, with Angus. Rebecca'll put you in the picture.'

'Right, I'll get myself clued up,' Meg nodded, and turned into her own office.

Rebecca, her senior staff nurse and chief support, was ready for her at a desk stacked with ominous piles of paper, notes and files. Dominating the paperwork, though, was a huge vase of glowing autumn flowers and berries.

'Wow!' Meg exclaimed. 'How absolutely super. Where do they come from?'

'From all of us. And welcome back.' Rebecca, whose hair was as dark as Meg's, but who was otherwise her opposite in looks, being tiny, plump and bouncy, eyed her uneasily.

Meg was touched by the welcome. 'They're gorgeous. We'll keep them here for everyone to enjoy.'

'No, they're for you to take home. Gosh, it's great to see you again.'

'It's great to see you, and to be here.' It was almost true, even if the feeling wasn't likely to last, and it certainly showed her what a mistake it would have been to walk out on her job. She smiled across the desk at Rebecca, genuinely if a little waveringly. This was her hospital, her office and her ward, and these were her friends. So she'd had an unhappy love-affair. So what?

In any case, it hadn't been unhappy. That was the trouble. The unhappiness came when it ended. Because it ended.

Come on, Meg Ashton, get stuck in, she told herself. Work, the great healer — or so they say. 'Duncan said something about the side-ward, and you'd put me in the picture,' she said.

'That's right. Priority number one for today. We've a new patient coming in any moment — of course, most of them are new to you; there's hardly anyone who hasn't been admitted since you left. However, I'll cover them later. The side-ward's new patient comes first, and I'm afraid she's going to be tricky. It's a girl, Janey Barton, she's seventeen and she's coming here from Intensive Care as soon as Dr Ritchie passes her fit to leave.' Nicola Ritchie was the anaesthetist who ran Intensive Care. 'Dr Ritchie's meeting Angus and Duncan, and Mr Ritchie, to confer over her.' Angus Henderson was the orthopaedic consultant on Meg's ward, while Andrew Ritchie, Nicola's husband, was the consultant in general surgery, and the cause of Rebecca's unease, since he happened also to be Rupert's chief.

Meg took in the implications at once. Just as Angus would be accompanied by his senior registrar, Duncan, so Andrew Ritchie would very likely be joined by Rupert, and they would all trail up together to the side-ward to see the patient satisfactorily installed. She straightened her shoulders irritably. So she might be going to encounter Rupert here on her own ward inside half an hour.

It didn't matter. It wasn't going to matter. She had to meet him some time. The sooner the better, perhaps.

And perhaps not. She sighed. She'd been hoping to postpone their first meeting for much longer than this.

'Janey was admitted yesterday afternoon,' Rebecca was saying, 'in the midst of bags of excitement and running about. They had a high old time in Cas. Janey had a suspected acute appendix, and her GP sent her in—he'd been on to Cas, they were expecting her. Well, her father was driving her in, and her mother was in the car too. So they crashed on the motorway, wouldn't you know? Probably he was driving too fast, panicking because his daughter was in so much pain.

'Anyway, the car went out of control, and the end of it was that all three of them arrived here in one ambulance. The father is in Intensive Care with nasty chest injuries, the mother, who was in the back, was luckily only badly bruised and shaken, but Janey now has a fractured tib and fib to add to her problems, poor soul.

'They had to have two teams in the theatre yesterday afternoon to see to her; Andrew Ritchie did the appendicectomy — she had a roaring inflamed appendix, only just missed peritonitis, they say — while Duncan saw to the fractures. They put her straight into Intensive Care, of course, but they're short of beds, as usual, so this morning they're having this get-together over her — Angus and Andrew Ritchie, plus Nicola Ritchie, natch, and also our new consultant, who's been around since Monday——'

'Help — I'd forgotten all about him. When does Angus actually finish?' asked Meg.

'Tomorrow. Had his final ward round yesterday, so you missed that. The new man came with him — very dishy, and bright with it, we all thought. Drew, his name is. Angus is being given a big sherry party in the boardroom this evening — your invitation's in that pile there. We accepted for you.'

Of all things, a boardroom party! Meg knew she should never have worn jeans. And Rupert would be bound to be there, so even if she managed to miss him this morning she'd have to face him this evening. She couldn't possibly get out of going, not Angus's retirement party. 'I'm sorry I missed his final round,' she said, annoyed with herself. Too wrapped up in her own misery, she thought, to think about anyone else, and so she'd overlooked Angus's retirement. He'd been a tower of strength to patients and staff, and to lose him from the ward would be to lose not only one of the most likeable and reliable surgeons in the hospital, but a friend, if not a father-figure. 'I hope you got him a special cake for tea yesterday?'

'We got him that cherry Genoa he always likes, and he seemed very happy with it,' said Rebecca. 'Anyway, you haven't missed him altogether. He'll be in tomorrow for his final list, so you can say goodbye then.'

'Any cherry Genoa left?'

'In the cupboard — about a third.'

'Right. Let's keep off it today, and then if he isn't in too much of a rush he can have some tomorrow. Talking of rush, back to this Janey girl, before we do the rest of the ward, and then I must try to clear this desk.'

'Yesterday we sent a fracture bed to the theatre for her, so she'll be coming back on that,' said Rebecca. 'Brenda's prepared the side-ward, the office are sending an extra nurse to special her — they swore she'd be fully trained and not a student.' Rebecca swallowed. Now came the bit Meg wasn't going to like. 'General surgery are monitoring her appendicectomy, so we'll have them in and out all day, I suppose.' 'Them' included Rupert, of course.

Meg shrugged it off, however. 'We can live with that, I reckon. Now tell me about the rest of the ward.'

Rebecca embarked on a series of case histories, and time fled by while Meg concentrated on the ups and downs, problems, triumphs and failures of the new occupants of what she always thought of as her ward. Mrs Mulgrue was one of the failures.

'Poor little Mrs Mulgrue is back in again,' Rebecca said. They'd all been fond of Chrissie Mulgrue. She was tiny, only just over five feet tall, very slim, with a mass of dark curls and a wide smile — or she had when Meg had last seen her.

'Well, that's not altogether unexpected, is it?' she commented. 'But I'm sorry to hear it. I thought she might be going to get away with it.'

'Me too. But her pain is worse, and now it's not just in her back, but down her leg.' Rebecca pulled a despairing face.

Chrissie Mulgrue had been discharged home to her large affectionate husband and her two energetic daughters of eight and ten just before Meg had left for her holiday. Three weeks earlier she'd been admitted with acute back pain, caused, Angus thought, by a tear to a disc, a ring of cartilage surrounding jelly, and lying between the vertebrae of the spinal column. If a disc tore, the jelly in the centre, the nucleus, could move forward into the vertebral canal, bringing pressure on to the nerves of the spinal cord and causing excruciating pain.

Chrissie had been nursed for two weeks flat in bed on pelvic traction. She'd had to wear a corset-like canvas belt round her hips, with straps leading to a pulley and weights at the end of the bed, tilted so that her head was lower than her heels. This was to relieve the pressure on the nerve by increasing the space between the vertebrae, and so give the disc a chance of returning to normal without surgery. If it had worked, that would have been the end of it. But evidently it hadn't, so Chrissie had come back into hospital for more investigations.

'What a shame,' Meg said. 'After those two miserable weeks in traction—and she was so good about it.'

'That's right, she was terrific. Hardly ever complaining, and whenever her husband came in with the children she was so cheerful and marvellous, and so fabulously jokey with them.'

'It must have been a huge strain on her, though—I remember the night staff said she had a quiet little weep sometimes, when she thought no one would notice.'

'I'm not surprised,' said Rebecca. 'I'd have been moaning and carrying on non-stop if I'd had to put up with all that. But during the day she never even murmured, and she did her exercises regularly as clock-work without being reminded, too. Things have changed now, I can tell you.'

'Oh, dear. How did she come back in?'

'She came to see Angus in Outpatients with this pain in her leg—she could hardly walk. So he brought her back in for a radiculogram, and that showed a prolapsed intervertebral disc, so Angus did a laminectomy last week.'

'So now he's removed the disc surgically, and I suppose she's back on another two weeks at least in bed.'

'That's right, and we're back to turning her every two hours of course,' said Rebecca.

'Yes, I see. But she's not doing too well?'

Rebecca shook her dark head. 'She's sort of collapsed emotionally — she's right down. It's finding herself back where she started after all these weeks, only worse, of course, because now she's had surgery and she has this wound, and dressings, and drainage tubes and all the rest of it. And she's lost all confidence in the outcome too, expecting the worst, absolutely convinced it's all going to go wrong again, nothing's going to be any good.'

Meg sighed. 'Oh, poor little Chrissie. I understand exactly how she feels, poor lamb.'

'Me too. But it isn't helping her one bit, of course. And, while her exercises are even more important now, she's not bothering about them in the way she did before. She doesn't make any effort to do them, she has to be reminded every hour or she just skips them, and anyway she doesn't exactly push herself. She's gone fatalistic — you know, nothing's going to go right for her, nothing's going to make any difference, it's all useless, so why invite more pain? I'm so glad you're back. You may be able to galvanise her — I certainly haven't been able to, but she always took a lot of notice of anything you said.'

Meg frowned. 'Well, I'll have a talk with her, if that's what you think, but I can't honestly believe it'll make much difference. In her shoes I'd feel pretty despairing myself. Oh, dear, I can't say I'm surprised we've got her back, but I do wish we hadn't. However, there it is. I'll do what I can. Now, who else is there?'

'More or less just the old faithfuls,' Rebecca told her. 'Nothing really changed on any of them. Young Timmy is still with us, but his parents have found a tutor for him, who comes in on alternate days to coach him for his A levels, and leaves him piles of work to get on with. So that's really great, and he's much less of a handful. More studious and a bit academic, and complaining about too much noise, would you believe? But it means he's much more manageable, and not at all the nuisance he used to be. And old Mr Black has achieved a rather perilous totter outside the ward — all along the corridor on his walking frame, and the physios have begun muttering about tackling the stairs next, so who knows? Even he may be discharged before Christmas; you never know.'

Meg sighed. 'I doubt it. And where to? That's going to be the next problem.'

'Think positively.' Rebecca grinned wickedly. This was a quote from Angus, often declaimed on the ward.

'How about thinking positively about getting ourselves across into the ward, before all the top brass descend on us?' said Meg. 'I'll be tied up for ages once this new patient arrives. Come on, it's not half nine yet. You do the medicines with Brenda, while I take myself round and meet all the new patients.' This activity enabled her to avoid thinking about the unwelcome prospect of encountering Rupert, and in fact he wasn't with the team who came to settle Janey Barton into the side-ward. She was sedated still, with tubes coming out everywhere, drips, and a ventilator on stand-by — it took five of them more or less half the morning to connect her up with her plumbing and electronics. She looked wan, vulnerable and deathly pale, and Meg's heart went out to her, as all her various anxieties dissolved into one overwhelming concern for this girl. Between them they had to pull her through.

'Apart from anything else, she could suddenly go into shock. Or bleed.' Meg looked across at Duncan, frowning as she worked out how she was going to manage. 'She'll have to have someone specialling her non-stop. The office were supposed to be sending us someone, but no sign so far, wouldn't you know? And no way can she be left.'

Duncan raised his eyes heavenwards. 'They promised to cover it,' he said. 'Angus refused to take her without extra cover, and Nicola backed him, saying she really ought to stay with them for another twenty-four hours, only they're so short of beds. You might have to make do with a third-year, I dare say, but they swore you'd get someone. Raise hell.'

'If no one appears within the next half-hour I certainly will,' said Meg. At that point she said goodbye to her own lunch-hour. She'd have a sandwich in the office. She'd be able to keep an eye on the side-ward then, and whoever she'd found to staff it, as well as begin to make inroads on the piles of paperwork leering at her from her desk. 'I'll eat on the hoof,' she told Rebecca. This was another of Angus's phrases, known as Angus-speak on the ward he'd dominated for more than twenty years.

Angus Henderson was small and wiry, and perpetually in transit — between Casualty, Outpatients, theatres or wards, often consuming *en route* varied forms of nourishment pressed anxiously on him by sisters, staff nurses, physios, secretaries and even — or so it was alleged — by social workers, not typically in the habit of extending a caring spirit towards staff or colleagues, but rather of reserving this emotion for patients — or clients, as they preferred to call them. Angus, though, seemed to be different, to have crossed some invisible barrier where he too was on the receiving end of benevolence. They'd even subscribed quite generously towards his retirement present. The ward had reeled from the shock.

The extra nurse for Janey Barton arrived at last, though Meg had to battle with the office to obtain her, and even then they could only offer her a third-year, they said. When she arrived, however, to Meg's relief, she seemed sensible and quietly competent, as well as familiar with the electronics, and Meg was able to leave her in the side-ward without too much anxiety — or not more than could be relieved by popping in and out every fifteen minutes.

Midday, and Rebecca stuck her head round the office door. 'What sandwiches do you want?' she asked. 'I'm going down now, with Brenda. The new girl's going as soon as we get back. Brenda'll take over. Now, there's a nice cream cheese and celery roll they've started doing — how about that?'

'Sounds fine. Thanks.'

'Apple? Banana? Yoghurt?'

'An apple, please,' said Meg. 'If I get time to run home, I can eat it in the car.'

'Right. Back in half an hour or so.' Rebecca shut the office door, and set off for the canteen.

Meg's lunch-hour disappeared without trace. There was a minor crisis in the ward, and as soon as that had been sorted out she took the opportunity of having a quiet chat with Mrs Mulgrue. 'So here you are back again with us,' she began. 'I am sorry to hear you've had such a rotten time.'

'Oh, Sister, how lovely—you're here again. I hope you had a good holiday.' Mrs Mulgrue summoned up a watery smile, but Meg could see at once that most of the fight had gone out of her. She spent more than half an hour at her bedside, talking to her and trying to reassure her that she really was going to improve and end up free from pain.

'You've had the surgery now, and you're almost over the worst. In a month from now, with any luck, you'll be home again and able to put all this behind you.'

Mrs Mulgrue, not unnaturally, looked unconvinced, as the two nurses arrived to turn her. They brought a message for Meg too. The third-year was worried, as the monitor in the side-ward was showing a different pattern.

Meg was worried too, and rang for the house surgeon, the ward's dogsbody, known to them all as Drip-Dry.

Drip-Dry said Janey Barton was all right, he thought. Nicola Ritchie had said the monitor might show that wave pattern within the next three to six hours. 'Want to watch the electrolyte levels, though, and where are the lab reports? Have they sent —? No, I suppose not. There hasn't really been time, even if they were trying. Chase them up, though, will you, Meg? And how about the catheters? Output?'

Meg told him, they both went on watching the monitor, and the third-year, enjoying herself immensely, drank it in.

Meg remained uneasy, and decided that she dared not leave the ward, even if she could find the time. She had little faith in Drip-Dry other than as a useful pair of hands. As such he was undoubtedly effective — skilful, gentle, deft. In the theatre, Duncan said, he was above average. But he was no sort of thinker, and as a scientist he rated below zero, in Meg's opinion, though Duncan said she was unfair. 'All right, he's not Mastermind, but he's careful and conscientious. Painstaking. Reliable, in his ponderous fashion.'

But Meg never liked relying on him, and she was thankful when Duncan appeared and she could ask him about the new wave pattern.

However, he too had been briefed by Nicola Ritchie, and agreed with Drip-Dry, though he at least was able to explain to Meg the thinking behind Nicola's opinion. The lab reports came in while he was in the office, and he looked through them and discussed treatment with Meg. Then they did a round of the main ward together, and afterwards, back in the office again, they had tea while Duncan wrote up the notes, brooded over X-rays, and filled in countless forms.

'No more of Angus's awful scratched hieroglyphics to try and decipher after this week,' Meg commented. 'We're going to miss him, though.'

'Place won't be the same without him,' Duncan agreed. 'But you'll get along with the new bloke, I'm sure — not that I've the faintest idea of the standard of his handwriting.' His own scrawl wasn't up to much, in any case, and Meg knew it was unlikely that the new man would be an exception to the general rule that doctors wrote like demented hooligans.

Duncan reached for his tea with his left hand while scrawling notes with his right. 'Any of that cherry Genoa on offer?'

'Sorry, I'm keping it for Angus tomorrow, in case he has time for a cuppa.'

The day had almost vanished, and Meg hadn't had a moment to dash home and collect something to wear this evening. She'd have to go in uniform, that was all. What did it matter? It might even, it occurred to her, be a good plan to meet Rupert looking her most stiff and starchy.

Duncan apparently followed her line of thought unerringly. 'I'll call in around six and collect you for the boardroom do,' he informed her.

'Oh — um — well, thanks. You don't have to, though. I shan't forget, and I do know the way.'

'I know you aren't going to cut Angus's party,' he agreed, his eyes on the notes he was continuing to write. 'But left to yourself you might be a little dilatory, it seems to me.'

Meg regarded his bent head with affection mixed with a good deal of irritation. Duncan and his wife were her closest friends in Halchester — she was godmother to their first-born, and a reliable baby-sitter. His present offer was meant kindly, she reminded herself. More than that, it was kind, and she shouldn't carp. If anyone needed her friends, she did. 'Well, thanks, anyway,' she said reluctantly, and distinctly ungraciously, she realised. To make up for this she added, 'How's Anne? Is she coming this evening?'

'She's fine. But we couldn't get a baby-sitter for tonight, so she won't be here, but she's coming tomorrow. You've heard about that, I suppose. The theatres, recovery-rooms, and Intensive Care are giving Angus a final send-off. It's to be in the empty ward, and afterwards there's a dinner party at the Ritchies'. You should have had an invitation — must be somewhere among all your bumf.'

'I found it. And I rang Nicola and thanked her and said I'd be there.' Meg's voice was sombre.

Duncan shot her a glance. 'Cheer up. You'll enjoy it when you get there, you know.' He read her expression with no difficulty. 'Yes, he's bound to be there, I should think. He's Andrew's senior registrar, after all.'

'I know I'm being silly,' Meg said weakly.

'In at the deep end, love. Easiest in the long run.'

'I suppose so.' It wasn't going to be easy, though. And she longed not to possess this stupid give-away face that Duncan, and no doubt other people too, could apparently read like large print. He obviously knew exactly how she was feeling. He was being kind and thoughtful, and she had to stop being so prickly and touchy, and accept his support.

'What are friends for?' he asked, taking the thought straight out of her head for the second time.

'Thanks,' she said, sounding astonishingly ungrateful, she realised as soon as she'd spoken. 'Sorry — I'm being awful. I just wish it were next week or next month or next year, and everyone had got used to the idea that Rupert and I aren't going around together any more, and found something else to be interested in.'

'I know,' he agreed. 'But that's why in at the deep end is a good plan. After two parties here in the hospital and the Ritchies' dinner they'll have had their fill ——'

'That's what I'm afraid of. Living through that.'

'Stiff upper lip, sweetie. You can do it. Anne and I'll be there to protect you too, and then after the weekend they'll have the new consultant to watch and talk about, and you and Rupert'll be old hat.'

'I do hope so. What's he like, the new man? He seems to have made a good impression on Rebecca.'

'First consultant post, apparently. He's from the Midland Accident Hospital, so he must know his stuff — been senior registrar in orthopaedics there. So he'll be the junior consultant, unlike Angus. But it shouldn't matter as far as we're concerned. I'd say he'd have plenty of clout. He certainly doesn't strike me as in any way a submissive type.'

'Orthopods seldom are, in my experience,' Meg rejoined, with a quick smile.

Duncan grinned. 'I dare say you have something there,' he agreed. 'Well, see you sixish, then.'

He was as good as his word, appearing a few minutes after the hour. Meg had just donned a fresh cap and renewed her make-up ready for the fray.

The party was already in full swing. The noise of it came to meet them as soon as they went through the double doors into the boardroom corridor.

'Seems half the hospital has beaten us to it,' Duncan commented, and then they were through the door and in the thick of it themselves. Duncan's hand came reassuringly under her arm, as Meg's eyes searched — unwisely, as she knew only too well — for Rupert.

Before she'd discovered him, though, the familiar figure of Angus Henderson came into sharp focus, unmistakably ploughing a determined furrow through the crowd towards them. As soon as she caught his eye he smiled broadly, raised his eyebrows as he dodged another animated group, and then he was with them.

'Welcome back, my dear. I'm delighted to see you.'

'I'm only so sorry I missed your final round yesterday,' Meg apologised.

'Of no consequence, none whatever. This is much more fun, eh?'

'This is really great,' Meg lied firmly. 'And I'm so thankful to be back in time for it.'

'Wouldn't have dreamt of having my leaving party without you, my dear. Would have had to tell them to postpone it if you hadn't been back, wouldn't I?'

'No, you wouldn't,' Meg said, with a wide smile.

'You think not? You underrate me, my dear.'

All this 'my dearing' and heavy Edwardian gallantry was, Meg recognised clearly, Angus's own way of being supportive. Like Duncan, he was making an effort to boost her morale, and it was sweet of him, even if it did mean that he was yet another of them who apparently knew everything there was to know about Rupert and herself.

'I'll get you a drink, Meg,' Duncan said. 'What about you, sir? Fill you up?'

'Not at the moment, no, thanks. But you go and get something for Meg, and then join us over by the fireplace, will you? I want to introduce her to my successor. Come along, my dear, let's make our way through the mob, if we can.'

Obediently Meg followed Angus across the room, willing herself not to allow her eyes to wander in search of anyone at all. But as they came nearer the knot of consultants grouped round the empty fire, they ceased to want to wander anywhere as, incredulous, she did a fast double-take. It couldn't be, surely? But it was. Duncan had told her the new man was called Drew, certainly, but it wasn't an uncommon name, and it hadn't crossed her mind that it could possibly be Jon. But there he was, of all people. His shoulders even broader, he stood there, four-square and unmistakable, and garbed in consultant's prosperous pin-stripe.

'Jonathan,' Angus was saying, 'I want to introduce you to someone who's going to be very important in your life here. This is Meg Ashton, the genius who runs our ward for us. Meg, this is Jonathan Drew, who's taking over from me.'

'Actually,' she said in a shaken voice, 'we've already met. But it was a long time ago,' she added hastily, in case it should turn out that he didn't remember her.

But he did.

'Meg,' he said, beaming. 'It is you? Yes, it is. You've — er — grown.' The dark eyes she remembered so well from all those years back were laughing at her in the way he had.

The years evaporated. 'Possibly,' she agreed, with the lift at the corner of her mouth he'd never forgotten.

'And changed in other ways too,' he added. His eyes sparked complicity, as they'd done so often before. 'Small world,' he remarked earnestly.

She nodded seriously. 'Long time no see,' she responded with due solemnity. The cliché game, which they'd played together in their irreverent youth. Her mouth quirked again, and she grinned delightedly. At that moment, all her problems were forgotten.

'I'll leave you two to do some catching up, then,' Angus told them. 'I ought to be circulating.'

'What on earth can you be doing in nursing, of all things?' Jon demanded., 'Weren't you going to read English Lit. at Oxbridge?'

'That was the general idea.' Meg was amazed that he remembered. 'All change, that was what happened. Dad was furious. In fact, he still hasn't come to terms with me nursing. From the way he refers to it, you'd think I spent my days in an old people's home, mopping up after the incontinent and making beds.'

'But what happened to all those plans for an academic career? If anyone was headed for Girton and a future in some ancient seat of learning it was you. So why here instead?'

You are what happened, Meg thought to herself. But no way could she come out with something like that. He'd be embarrassed, and so would she. In those far-off days she'd been no more than a schoolgirl he'd teased, and occasionally, out of politeness to her father, escorted. But what was she to tell him?

She'd have to produce a half-truth. 'It was meeting you at the hospital.'

'Meeting me at the *hospital*?' He stared, obviously lost, but then his eyes glinted with humour. 'Expound,' he ordered pedantically.

The expression, and the voice in which he uttered it, was lifted straight from her father. Professor Ashton at his most rigorous. And to the life.

Meg chuckled appreciatively. Apart from anything else, Jon had always been such fun.

That same enchanting chuckle—Jonathan Drew

recognised it instantly. And what an astonishingly beautiful young woman she'd turned into. The gawky schoolgirl had vanished, and the new Meg Ashton took him aback. So did her next remarks.

'The hospital and the life you all led grabbed me, possessed me, from then on. And I knew it was the only world for me. I don't suppose you had any idea how different it was from everything I'd known before — school, the campus, students, dons' sherry parties. Not to mention dons' backbiting. Hospital was an entirely different world, and I wanted more. I wanted to stay in it. Of course, I'd felt rebellious for a long while, but until then basically I'd only experienced academic life. At the hospital it was people with real problems that had to be solved, while on the campus there was never-ending drama, but suddenly I realised it was all prefabricated. I saw this clearly, all at once, and I've never regretted — in fact I'm still thankful — that I did see it. And I owe it to you.' She looked straight into his eyes, as she'd always done. 'You were worth ten of those querulous dons, you know. I saw it so plainly. You and the hospital changed my life, and I'm grateful. So now you know why I'm here. All due to you.'

'I'm stunned,' he told her. He would have gone on, but Duncan reappeared, with a brimming glass for Meg.

'Sorry to have been so long, but I kept getting caught up,' he apologised.

'I didn't notice the time,' Meg said truthfully. 'Thanks, anyway.'

'It's what you asked for, neither more nor less.'

Since Duncan could always be trusted, this meant he had brought her straight tonic with no hidden kick in it. After this bash she had to drive home, she had reminded him as they'd walked over to the boardroom. He had at once offered to drive her himself, but then she would have the problem of getting in the following morning, she'd pointed out. He had given in, but he was obviously disappointed, and she'd realised that he had been planning to pour strong drink into her to ease the pain of meeting Rupert. Well, it was a nice idea. In some ways she could think of nothing more useful than getting sloshed. Not, however, in the boardroom at Angus's retirement party, Rupert or no Rupert.

Duncan was offering to fetch Jon a refill.

'Thanks, that'd be very kind.' He drained his glass and handed it over.

'G and T?' asked Jon.

'No. I'm on straight tonic—I've promised to drive Angus home. He can hardly stay on the wagon at his own party.'

'Lord, another of you! Half the room seems to be on Perrier or tonic. I don't know what things are coming to these days. Right, on my way.'

'Half the room, indeed! He means me, actually,' Meg explained. 'I have to drive home after this too.'

'That's straight tonic, is it?' asked Duncan. 'You look as if you could do with something a bit stronger inside you—why don't I drive you as well as Angus?'

Another of them deciding that what she needed was a stiff drink. But Jon at least couldn't know anything about Rupert.

Here she was wrong. Angus had briefed him on

Meg's collapsed relationship with Rupert. 'You've a jewel of a ward sister in Meg Ashton,' he'd told him. 'But if you can manage to go a bit easy on her when she comes back from this holiday it might pay off in the long term. She's just had what was once called a disappointment in love — she and the senior registrar from general surgery split up just before she departed, so she may not be quite her usual self at first. Tread gently, if you can — she's a girl worth keeping.'

'I'll bear it in mind,' Jon had promised, though then, of course, he hadn't guessed this was Meg they were talking about. Now he wanted to know more.

She was busily explaining about needing her own car in the morning to come to the hospital. He wasn't going to have any of that. 'I'll collect you,' he said. 'I'm quite reliable — I won't let you down, or be late or anything. You can trust me.'

She could trust him forever, to the ends of the earth and beyond, she knew that. She'd always known it. But she continued to protest. 'Jon, it's sweet of you, but you can't possibly——'

'Oh, yes, I can. No problem. Now stop arguing like this; give me your glass and I'll get you a real drink. Something tells me you need it.'

'Well, thanks, it would be nice,' she agreed — weakly, she realised, but somehow with Jon it was different. She had no need to keep up her defences.

'Tell you what, why don't you come on with us to Long Barn for dinner?' he was saying. 'That'll be the thing. I'm taking Angus and Jean there after this is over — they can't just creep away home, far too flat. Do come. He'd like it, I'm sure. He's been singing your praises, telling me how incredibly lucky I am to have this super ward sister. So do come.'

The way he was looking at her took her back ten years, and did unexpected things to much more than her morale. 'If you're sure,' she began uncertainly.

'Of course I'm sure. I'll check it with Angus, to set your mind at rest, if you like, but he'll be pleased as Punch.'

'It would be a fantastic end to the evening — but I'd have to go home and change first, I'm afraid.' How wrong she'd been this morning, but who would have thought it possible that Jon would be talking to her here in St Mark's this evening? 'I've only jeans and trainers here — not quite Long Barn gear.'

'Maybe not — I heard the place is the tops, so I'm booked in there for my first weeks here. So far I've found it all it was cracked up to be. Now, let's see. What I'll do is drive you home as soon as Angus has made his speech, come back here for him and Jean — that'll give them time to say their goodbyes to everyone — and then collect you again in about half an hour, with them, and we'll go straight on to Long Barn. Right, that's settled. Now I'll get you that drink.'

CHAPTER TWO

JON'S spirits lifted. Dinner with Meg as well as the Hendersons would be fun, a much more attractive proposition than the duty meal he had been anticipating. Of all things to happen, right out of the blue! To come to this new and hitherto unknown hospital and discover Meg — and not only find her here, but in post as his ward sister. What a beautiful creature she'd turned into, too. A far cry from the leggy, coltish schoolgirl, with her clumsy gaucheries and her sudden offbeat, zany charm.

Here she stood opposite him, almost his own height — or at any rate up to his chin — even if only about half his width, bless her. Slim-waisted in sister's dark blue, immaculate, a crisp cap perched at a highly becoming angle on the same short dark hair, though these days some master hand had cut it for her.

They'd a load of catching up to do. Years, after all, had gone by — ten years, it must be. Something was wrong, though. All at once she was tense, uptight, watchful. That was it, watchful. On guard. Why?

Jon searched his mind for clues. Angus had already briefed him about his new ward sister. He'd praised her to the skies, told Jon he was immensely lucky to inherit her, and to be sure to hang on to her, no matter what.

No matter what — that was it. Angus had mentioned a recent disastrous love-affair, had asked him to go gently with her to start with. Some surgeon here at St Mark's had dropped her flat — and rather publicly, too.

It would have to wait. They were about to be interrupted.

'Hi, Meg, you're looking well. Won't you introduce me?'

The newcomer, Jon saw, was darkly handsome and expensively suited, slightly built, probably in his thirties. And Meg had stiffened her spine and was even more rigid and on guard.

'Of course,' she agreed, her voice cool, giving nothing away. 'Rupert Cornwell, Jon, senior registrar in general surgery. Mr Jonathan Drew, who's succeeding Angus.' As of course you perfectly well know, she thought. That's why you're here.

Two pairs of eyes met warily. Jon was asking himself if this Rupert Cornwell could be the surgeon Angus had warned him about, who had let Meg down. Whoever he was, he was making polite, welcoming noises, and enquiring what hospital Jon came from.

'The Midland Accident Hospital,' Jon told him.

'An outstanding centre, I've always heard.'

'It has quite a reputation, yes. And not unjustified, I'd say. A good place to work, too.' Apart from his suspicions, Jon didn't take to Rupert. He was a little too smooth, too well turned-out, and trying too hard to ingratiate himself with a new consultant. Climbing the ladder rather too blatantly. And was he, or was he not, the man who had hurt Meg?

He must be. She was still as stiff as a poker, and her eyes, previously friendly and open, the eyes of the eager, trusting girl he'd known all those years ago, had gone stony. She was on guard, not a doubt of it, and, whatever had happened between them, she wasn't over it. She was suffering. Angus had been right.

No one was going to treat his Meg like that and get away with it. What might have happened next could have been interesting, if not downright dangerous, but—perhaps fortunately—they were interrupted again.

The chairman of the medical committee banged on the table for silence. It was time for the presentation.

The moment the speeches were over, Jon hustled Meg out of the boardroom, along the passage and out into the car park, determined she'd hold no more of these upsetting conversations with Rupert Cornwell. Once he had her installed in the front seat of his Audi, she had to concentrate on giving him directions to the little riverside terrace of eighteenth-century cottages where she lived, overlooking the jetty.

'What a super spot.' He was entranced. 'You must have been extraordinarily lucky to get hold of this, surely?'

'Isn't it fantastic?' Meg agreed. 'I love it. I took it over from one of the physios who's moved up north—it more or less fell into my hands, would you believe?'

'The views are quite breathtaking.' His eyes travelled the broad swaths of the river Hal as it meandered across the wide marshes bordering the estuary.

At that moment Meg almost unburdened herself. She was on the verge of telling him the entire story. How it was this, her beloved cottage by the river, that had drawn her back to St Mark's and her job, when all her instincts had been urging her to flee to the furthest ends of the country and never see Rupert or anyone else at St Mark's ever again.

What had brought her back had been a mixture of emotions. Pride was one, allied to natural combativeness. Why should she have to abandon everything she cared for simply because Rupert had lost interest in her? Devotion to her little cottage, the first home she had ever owned, was another, and perhaps the strongest.

Jon would understand exactly how she felt, she was sure of this. He'd always known how much she missed not having a proper home or any family life.

Her father, as an impecunious young lecturer, had married, hurriedly and unwisely, everyone agreed, the prettiest of his students. At the time, Meg's mother had been wildly in love with her tall, handsome and academic husband, and to start with she had transformed herself joyfully into a dedicated wife and mother — to no one's surprise, Meg had arrived during the first year, within the honeymoon period of what was later to become, perhaps inevitably, a disastrous marriage. Ecstasy was replaced by resentment and, finally, despair, the couple divorced before Meg left junior school, and had in fact been leading entirely separate existences since she was about four.

Her mother took off, rapturously again, for a new marriage in a new country, and left Meg behind with her father. He had never been in any way domestic — it had been one of his wife's many complaints — and within the year he had sold the house on the outskirts of the town where Meg had been brought up, and moved back to a flat on the campus, where his secretary was on the spot and could organise mundane details like cleaning and a constant supply of food.

From then on, the nearest person Meg had to a mother was this capable and hardworking woman, unfailingly kind as well as efficient, but with a house of her own and two teenage children to look after. Real family life was non-existent, her father became vaguer and more distant with every year that passed, and Meg, in default of anything better, threw herself passionately into her studies and the joys of English literature. She did brilliantly — until she encountered Jon and hospital life. Then at last she rebelled, threw the school into uproar and infuriated her father by, as he put it, 'throwing her future away' to become a student nurse.

Owning and moving into No. 1, Ferry Cottages had been the fulfilment of a dream, and no way, she found, could she abandon it. She turned confidingly to Jon, ready to explain all this.

But then she remembered he had to go back to the hospital and collect Angus and Jean, while she hurried indoors and changed into something suitable for Long Barn. 'Will you be able to find your way back to St Mark's?' she asked instead.

'I turn left at the fork back there, and left again into the main road, right? After that I know it.'

'That's it. See you shortly, then. Thanks for the lift, and the invitation too. A meal in Long Barn is a high spot around here, you know.' Four short weeks ago Rupert had taken her there for her birthday.

When they arrived there this evening it was, as ever, crowded to its ancient rafters — it was easily the most popular place for miles around. Jon had booked a table, though, and they were led across the restaurant towards a round table in the window.

To Meg's startled dismay there, only two tables away, was Rupert with Sally, his blonde bombshell, all got up in exotic purple drapes.

Nothing whatever to be done, she told herself. Just grin and bear it. Keep your cool, and don't react. Show nothing. Nil.

Angus was horrified. He'd spotted the vision almost at the same moment as Meg, and he swept a keen eye round to see if there was by any chance an empty table in a distant corner that he could suddenly decide would do them far better. But there wasn't often an empty table at Long Barn in the evening, and they were by no means early.

Jon, who had picked up Rupert's unwelcome presence almost as fast as Angus, was scanning the room as thoroughly. No one needed to tell him that the luscious blonde in floating purple chiffon must be Meg's replacement. Short of ejecting the two of them, though, there seemed no useful action he could take.

Angus, however, a fast worker and a quick thinker, gained them time. He took Jean affectionately by the arm, tenderly, his head bent towards her lovingly. The words he hissed in her ear were not loving but demanding—not for the first time. 'Get Meg out of here fast, and don't come back too soon. I need time.'

A theatre sister of an earlier vintage, Jean responded as she would have done at the operating table twenty years earlier. Hers not to reason why.

'I wonder if you'd order for me, dear?' she enquired sweetly of her husband. 'I think after all I'd really rather like to tidy up a bit. Meg won't mind coming with me, will you? I'm not sure I remember exactly where the cloakroom is.'

'Of course,' Meg said enthusiastically. 'What a good idea.' A chance to collect herself, to prepare for the ordeal ahead. She turned almost before the words were out, and led the way across the restaurant at what amounted to a fast trot.

'I suppose,' Jon enquired, his lip curling, 'that purple outfit covers Meg's successor?'

'I'm afraid so,' Angus said unhappily.

'What a *fool*. Dropping Meg for—for that bit of window-dressing.'

'Rupert's never been exactly what one would call far-sighted.' Angus shook his head. 'Unfortunately, however misguided he is, it does somewhat take the gilt off the gingerbread to have them in full view for our little celebration.'

'I'll see if I can fix it,' said Jon. 'After all, I'm a resident here, so I ought to be able to move a mountain or two, wouldn't you say?' He departed across the room with a long-legged, purposeful stride. Angus, always an accomplished delegator, sat down and immersed himself peaceably in the yard-wide menu.

Jon came back. 'They'll serve us in my sitting-room upstairs,' he said. 'It seemed the sensible way out—they're not likely to have another table for half an hour. We'll say we found it too crowded and noisy, shall we?'

'Right. It'll be much nicer to be a bit more secluded, after that mob in the boardroom.' Angus winked cheerfully.

'Shall we wander out, and pick up Jean and Meg in the foyer?'

'Let's do that,' Angus agreed.

The evening, Meg thought thankfully as she lay in bed on the verge of sleep, had turned out all right in the end. What a mercy Angus had found the restaurant too noisy! It had surprised her at the time, since normally he took crowds and crashes and argument and chatter in his stride. Bless him, he must be getting old. Of course, he had had a fearfully long day, and he'd done the rounds in the boardroom, talking to everyone. No wonder he felt like a bit of peace and quiet at the end of the day. And dinner in Jon's sitting-room upstairs at Long Barn had been a delight — that should teach her not to panic too soon. Over nothing, too. Life went on without Rupert.

Tomorrow there'd be the big party in the empty ward upstairs, followed by the Ritchies' dinner. Rupert would be at both, but Meg refused to worry about it. She'd survived this evening. Not merely survived, in fact; a good deal of it she'd really enjoyed. It had been fun with Jon and Angus and Jean. They'd had a super time. And tomorrow would be her second day back. Jon was coming to fetch her, they'd drive into that car park together, and then there'd be that poor Janey in the side-ward to sort out — and what had Rebecca said about old Mr Black on his walking frame? That he'd got as far as the corridor? She drifted off to sleep, and didn't rouse until her alarm went off.

Under the shower, she pondered what to wear. She wasn't going to be caught a second time with only jeans at the hospital, and she certainly couldn't continue to treat the new orthopaedic consultant as her personal chauffeur.

A vision in flamboyant purple assaulted her inner eye. Beat that, Meg Ashton, a small voice dictated.

All right, I will, she informed the shower curtain. Back in her bedroom, she extracted the most dramatic outfit she possessed from her wardrobe — floating muslin with the skirt cut into points, a wisp of a chemise with ribbon straps, and a loose overshirt, patterned with cascading water-lilies and reeds in sultry Monet colours.

'So you're going to waft into St Mark's at eight a.m. in this?' she asked the cupboard door. Hardly. She'd be hopelessly overdressed, and people would mutter to one another that she was going to all lengths to try and get Rupert back. She reached into the wardrobe again, and shook out the pleats of a suit even Rupert, who normally went for stunning colour — no doubt he'd been entranced by last night's purple chiffon — had admitted did things for her. The beige silk pleats, he'd told her, swayed as she moved in the most enticing manner, and the long tunic top — that summer's line — outlined her breasts and hips so promisingly.

Well, it had been a summer filled with promise. But it was gone, finished.

Oh, God.

Stop it, she told herself. Dress and get down those stairs. She couldn't be late and keep Jon waiting about while she had a good cry in her bedroom.

In the pink and green kitchen overlooking the bend in the river, she tipped muesli into one of her Italian pottery bowls, bought that summer to match the kitchen, not from Tuscany but from the reject stall in Halchester market. With Rupert, damn it. Angrily she cut a slice of wholemeal bread, slid it into the toaster, and started the coffee.

In the big kitchen of their Victorian house in Creek Road, Nicola and Andrew Ritchie were also drinking their coffee. Since Andrew was a surgeon and Nicola an anaesthetist, breakfast was not exactly a haven of peace, more a medley of telephone calls. This morning, one of the callers was Jean Henderson.

'I'm sure you must have thought about this already, Nicola, but I just thought maybe a word would be useful. About Meg Ashton—I'm sure Rupert is bound to be coming this evening; I do realise he's Andrew's senior registrar, and you can hardly not—'

'No, I don't see how we can, though I'd like to,' said Nicola. 'But at least it isn't going to be their first meeting—I saw them talking together quite amicably at the boardroom do for Angus. I'll certainly put them as far apart as I can, though—we're having a sit-down meal; I thought you'd all have had enough of standing about balancing food and drink.'

'If you could possibly put them at opposite ends of the table, then, and either Angus or me near Meg, we can see he doesn't get much chance to upset her. And Jon Drew is already proving an absolute tower of strength. Oddly enough, he and Meg know each other from way back—when he was a houseman, I think. Angus is so chuffed about it. They're going to make a super team, he thinks, and he's feeling much more relaxed now about handing over.'

'Shall I put Meg next to Jon, then?'

'That would be splendid.'

'I'll do that, then. See you later.' Nicola reached for her list and began rearranging her table.

Andrew came off the other line. 'More coffee?'

'Yes, please. That was Jean Henderson on my line. She's worried about tonight, wanting me to put Meg as far away from Rupert as I could.' Nicola sighed. 'I know he's a good surgeon——'

'And a nice chap,' Andrew said firmly. 'Apart from his womanising. But Meg shouldn't have expected the affair to last—damn it all, we all know Rupert, including her.'

'She certainly told everyone she knew it would be short-lived,' Nicola agreed. 'But I expect she found she'd got in deeper than she'd bargained for. And personally I think it was heartless of him to drop her like that just when they were supposed to be going on holiday. And so publicly, flaunting that blonde under her nose. That's when my opinion of him dropped below zero.'

'I did remonstrate with him over that,' said Andrew. 'I told him he might have waited a bit and done it more tactfully, but he said Sally was obsessing him, and it would have been sheer pretence to have gone away with Meg. She would have known everything was wrong between them, he maintained, and that would have been much worse than just cancelling the whole plan.'

'A nice theory, I must say. Leaves him free to do exactly what he wants. I suppose there's not the slight-est chance we could somehow uninvite him this evening? Could you simply be honest, and say Meg'll be here, and so it would be better if he wasn't?'

'I know what he'd say to that. They're the best of friends, and Meg understands the situation completely. Which no doubt she does, poor lass. She's just having problems living with it. But I'll see what I can think up—I rather agree with you. He went too far,' Andrew finished.

CHAPTER THREE

FLINGING her mohair serape round her silken shoulders, and luckily unaware of these plans made on her behalf, Meg stepped out into a misty, autumnal morning, locked the front door behind her, and sailed down the path to the front gate precisely as Jon's white Audi drew up.

He was at the wheel, looking this morning every inch the consultant, entirely changed from the rumpled, untidy boy she used to know. His broad shoulders encased in smooth dark pin-stripe, he radiated authority, and she wondered with a sense of shock how she had managed to be so relaxed and friendly with him last night. He was the new consultant, and he looked it.

But he grinned at her with the same slant to his wide mouth and the wicked gleam in his eye that had shattered her humdrum existence all those years ago. 'How about playing hookey?' he enquired. 'Neither of us seems exactly dressed for the hurly-burly of a hard day in the theatre, or the wards, so how about taking off? Nipping up to London on the motorway, say, lunch at Chez Nico, perhaps take in a gallery and after that a show and a late supper. How about it? And we turn up tomorrow looking as if butter wouldn't melt. No one would dare ask what happened to yesterday.'

'What a super idea.' This was the sudden joyous

42

madness of the boy she'd known, and she met the dark eyes with all her barriers down. 'Can we have champagne?'

'Of course. Goes without saying. You look terrific, by the way — in that outfit only champagne could possibly pass your lips.'

She glowed. Felt invincible. 'I'm on! Turn right for the motorway.'

'I might just take you at your word,' Jon told her. The dark eyes held hers, and she read in them an unmistakable awareness that jolted her. She had no idea how to deal with whatever it was that had suddenly erupted between them. 'Oh, dear,' she said hastily, turning her head away, 'please don't. Duty calls, worse luck.'

'You don't feel you might turn your back on it for once?' he queried.

'Not really, I'm afraid. I've got a ward to run, blow it. Anyway, it's Angus's final party this evening. That's why I'm all got up like this.'

'We could have been back in time for Angus's party,' he said mildly. 'And I'm not officially on call until Monday. That's when my appointment starts — until then I'm a mere visitor, hanging around as the whim takes me. It would have been fun, you know.'

Meg knew it would. Quite likely more than fun. But she was thankful to see he'd turned safely left for the hospital, not right for the motorway, London and champagne.

The party was, as they all knew it would be, a huge success. Unlike the boardroom party, it absorbed all-comers, from cleaners and porters to consultant surgeons and anaesthetists. It never lost impetus, since it was constantly charged with fresh blood as staff of every age and seniority dropped in before their stint in the operating theatres or Casualty, before or after duty.

Meg was far too busy chatting to be sad. Yet the consciousness of Rupert's presence in the ward never left her. She knew exactly where his dark head was, outlined for her against half a hundred others, exactly where he stood — in theatre overalls, he had evidently come straight from surgery and presumably intended to return there.

The evening wore on. There were speeches and another presentation to Angus, flowers for Jean, and then at last the party began to break up, though a few stalwarts remained, scoffing the last of the food.

The Ritchies left, with Angus and Jean, and Jon materialised at Meg's shoulder. 'I'll give you a lift to the Ritchies',' he said. 'Are you about ready for off?'

'Sure,' she told him.

'I just need a couple of words with the switchboard. I can ring from the theatres' phone on the way down.'

They went together down one flight, and Jon made for the wall telephone.

'I'll go on,' Meg said. 'I can pop into the cloakroom and tidy up, then meet you at the foot of the stairs, by the side-door to the car park. OK?'

'Fine. With any luck I shan't be long.' He picked up the telephone.

Meg surveyed his broad back, found it curiously reassuring. She was glad to be beginning the next stage of the evening with him safely by her side, and she descended the next flight of stairs feeling quite cheerful. Perhaps she was going to enjoy this evening after all.

On the landing between flights she paused. There was no one about. She didn't really need to plod along to the cloakroom. She could check her make-up here on the landing. She took out her compact, scrutinised her face, renewed her lipstick, tidied her eyebrows, smoothed back her dark hair. She'd do.

She loitered down the next flight. On the stairs above, there was a sudden rush of footsteps, and she turned, expecting Jon.

But it was Rupert.

She couldn't help it. Her gaze homed in joyously on the familiar form, still in green theatre overalls.

'Meg. There you are.' He smiled the smile that never failed to entrance her. 'At last. You've been avoiding me all evening, you know. Don't think I haven't noticed. So why? What's bugging you? What have I done?'

She didn't know what to say. The last thing she'd expected was that he'd come right out in the open and challenge her like this. She'd supposed, in fact, that he'd be thankful not to be bothered by her. She played for time. 'What do you mean avoiding you?' Wasn't that what he wanted her to do?

'Every time I came anywhere near you, you took off. I began to think I must be infectious or something.'

'Don't be silly.' That at least was easy.

'You have been avoiding me, Meg. You know you have, sweetie — be honest. I thought we were friends, you and I.' Brown velvety eyes caressed her, in the same old way, and almost undid her.

'I thought so too.' Much, much more than friends, but nothing would induce her to admit that sad truth. If only his eyes, his soft eyes that could be so gentle and loving, if only these eyes weren't undoing all her resolution, she'd have been able to answer him in the way he deserved. In the way she'd planned.

'You and I had so much going for us, sweetie, and I was sure we'd always be friends, no matter——'

Suddenly he'd blown it. He'd gone too far. His eyes were still making love to her, Meg thought furiously, while his lips were spelling out not truth but lies. He was trying to put her in the wrong, to pretend that he'd done nothing to upset her in any way, that she'd just, on no grounds whatever, decided to avoid him. He was behaving as if she'd deliberately picked a childish quarrel with him, while he'd done nothing. He stood there, a misunderstood male, hurt and loving. It was too much.

'Friends?' she exploded. 'I thought so too. But what sort of friend is it who cancels a holiday planned for months the day before it's due to start? Did you give a single thought to what I was supposed to do with my three weeks? Of course you didn't. And you call that being *friends*?'

'Meg, I—I realise I——' He didn't know what to say.

She'd wrong-footed him. Clearly, he was taken aback by her anger. He'd expected her, she saw, to jump at the chance of making up with him, even if she had to crawl. Well, she wasn't going to—or not yet, at any rate, though how long she could keep this up she didn't dare forecast. She was on sure ground, though. He had let her down; there was no getting away from it. So let him work that out. 'You didn't give one single thought to me and what I was going to do. As far as you were concerned, I simply didn't exist. And you stand here and talk to me about friendship?' She had made the word sound like an insult, she thought, momentarily pleased with herself. He was eyeing her warily now. Good. So he should.

'Look, Meg,' he began, clearly uncomfortable, she was glad to see, 'I do realise I let you down. It was atrocious of me. I can't imagine what got into me. Looking back, I think I must have been mad. What happened, I suppose, was— Oh, sweetie, I don't know—it just suddenly seemed impossible to—I mean, I—'

What he meant Meg saw, had always seen, with painful clarity. It had been part of the hurt of it. It just suddenly seemed impossible to Rupert to go anywhere and leave his latest girlfriend, Sally, behind.

Meg understood this, that was the awful part, and in one corner of her mind she sympathised. Sally had appeared and bowled him over, and from that moment on he'd been totally blind to anything or anyone but Sally. At that point, Meg was well aware, she herself hadn't existed. Now, though, nearly a month later, he'd calmed down, was back to his normal self, and he wanted, apparently, to pick up where they'd left off. Or thereabouts. Was he proposing to drop Sally this time round, and start up again as if nothing had happened with dear old Meg, waiting loyally in the wings? Was that the programme?

A glimpse of the promised land? Or not? If only she knew.

Perhaps, though, he was intending to run them both. For Rupert, of course, it wouldn't be for the first time. St Mark's had often watched, fascinated, laying bets, while Rupert pirouetted classily between two deluded women.

Deluded. Meg's lip curled. Exactly. No way was she going to be part of any set-up like that. It was all very well, though. She might decide to turn her back and walk away, but there was another girl inside her only too eager to be deluded. Just give her the chance! She only wanted Rupert back — at whatever price.

She saw clearly that she ought to walk away from Rupert now, this minute. And stay away. But this other girl inside her head wanted to stay with him forever. Put her arms round him, and feel his come round her, in the old familiar way.

What would have happened next, which of the two girls inside her would have won, she never found out. Another set of footsteps came pounding down the stairs.

Jon.

'Meg, I'm so sorry to have kept you hanging about like this. There were one or two problems.'

'It doesn't matter one bit.' It had been decided for her. And just as well, as it seemed she couldn't trust herself in any way. 'We're off to the Ritchies',' she explained hastily to Rupert. 'See you there, I expect.'

'Er — no, actually — um — not.' Rupert grasped, belatedly, why Andrew had unexpectedly asked him, this morning, to hold the fort at St Mark's instead of joining them for dinner. 'Enjoy yourselves,' he said sulkily. He turned on his heel and stamped away upstairs again.

Meg's eyes followed him, and her heart twisted.

Jon watched them both. He didn't like it at all.

As Meg sat beside him in the Audi, and then next to him at the Ritchies' dining-table in their great bay-windowed room overlooking the creek and the spreading marshes, he liked it less and less. For while she talked and laughed, kept her head and carried on long discussions that eventually arrived at intelligent conclusions, he could feel her pain.

They sat shoulder to shoulder, consuming Nicola's stuffed green peppers followed by her casserole of venison with redcurrant and orange, succeeded in due course by a marvellous edifice of honey and ginger ice-cream on crisp meringue topped by whipped cream and almonds. Meg duly praised the melting mouthfuls, and admired the flowers — a low arrangement in the middle of the huge round table of pale yellow dahlias and vivid Michaelmas daisies, surrounded by pungent spiky juniper. She played up indulgently to Angus's truly Edwardian gallantry, which became steadily more gallant with every glass of Andrew's soft fruity claret he downed. But all the while Jon was registering the steady misery behind the too glib chatter. This agony had not been there earlier. It dated from the moment he'd found her talking to Rupert on the stairs, he knew that. What had happened then? What had been said in those few short minutes while he'd been on the telephone?

Whatever it had been, it had devastated her.

At the end of the evening he dropped her off at her cottage before driving Angus and Jean home. Throughout the short drive he seemed abstracted and hardly spoke, so that Meg thanked him hurriedly for the lift, said goodbye quickly to Angus and Jean, and ran up her garden path to the privacy of her own home, where at last she'd be able to let go.

She gave a short, embittered laugh as she shut the front door behind her. It was the alternative to a long wail of despair.

At the end of this hard day, Jon's offhand silence had been the last blow, when she'd been imagining that with him she was as safe as ever. He was probably the only person in the world to whom she could have confided, not so much the pain, but the mess and muddle of her ever-changing feelings about Rupert. She could have told Jon about her uncertainties. About her love that refused to die.

But he hadn't been ready to listen. Why should he have been? There must be plenty going on in his life without adding her stupid love-affairs to it. He had, after all, his new job and a new hospital with new people, as well as a previous existence, quite unknown to her, in the Midlands from which he'd just come. One thing was for sure: she certainly wasn't the centre of his stage. But then she never had been., In the past it hadn't mattered. The trouble was, she wasn't the centre of anyone's stage.

Oh, for Pete's sake! She stamped upstairs and ran a bath. Pull yourself together, you wet hen, she scolded herself. Who in their right mind wants centre stage?

Particularly if that means sharing it with Rupert. Listen, micro-mind. You can live without Rupert. What's more, you're going to. You're going to break with him, and you're going to do it all by yourself.

You're a big girl now, and you don't need Jon to hold your hand while you do it.

This evening she'd been right round the twist. Just because she'd met Rupert and had a brief and wholly unsatisfactory conversation with him, she'd allowed her evening to be ruined.

She'd spent the evening refusing to admit what was staring her in the face. That was what had thrown her, that was why leaving Rupert behind at St Mark's had been so shattering. Somewhere inside her she had known that that short talk on the stairs had been her final break with him. If she had any guts at all. The end had come, and she had to accept it.

Earlier on, on the stairs, Rupert had deliberately opened a trap and waited for her to gallop headlong and lovingly into it. That was what their conversation had been about. When he'd accused her of avoiding him, he had been leading up to the big reconciliation scene. On his terms.

Until now, whatever else had gone wrong, he'd been honest with her. 'You do understand, Meg,' he'd said, right at the beginning, 'you do understand I don't go in for permanence, don't you? I'm not into the settling down, mortgage, marriage and hordes of kids scenario. Not for years yet. Not until I've landed a consultant post, if then. I'm not the faithful unto death type.'

He could say that again!

'You're totally fascinating, you know that?' he'd carried on. 'And I adore being with you. But nothing lasts forever. So is that all right with you? Not much, I'm afraid, but all I have to offer. I'd hate to hurt you, love; that's the last thing I'd ever want to do.'

Fine words, she thought. And mostly true, too. Except that, when it came to it, he hadn't cared whether he hurt her or not.

Blind to it, of course. He'd been thinking about Sally, and no one else. Even so, by his standards, he'd played fair. He played by his own rules, admittedly. But she'd accepted them, with her eyes open. It was her own fault that when the end actually came she couldn't take it.

All right, so she couldn't take it. What did that mean? Simply that she'd be a thousand and one different sorts of lunatic if she let him start up with her again, for a repeat performance. Because he'd altered the rules. Their relationship might have ended long before she was ready for it, but while it had been on she had been the only woman in his life. Now there was Sally. He'd said nothing about ending anything with her.

Meg climbed out of the bath and towelled herself, more alert than ever. Sleep would be impossible. She pulled on her pink towelling robe and descended to the kitchen to make tea. Only she was far too full of Nicola's mouth-watering meal to have room for even a few sips of tea. Or coffee. She didn't smoke, but a cigarette would be just the job. Only there wasn't one in the cottage.

Was what Rupert was planning now going to involve running her and Sally both? That was what he'd meant by being friends, perhaps. Sally and Meg, both of them Rupert's dear friends. Quite likely he thought of taking her out on the evenings Sally was on duty.

So did he intend to leap into her bed as well as Sally's? Or would he take her chastely to the theatre and a meal only? Sally for bedding, dear old Meg for a quiet, relaxing evening and a good meal.

'I thought we were friends.'

Huh! She wasn't going to wear it. She'd find it unbearable, far more painful than the clean break she'd already agonised over. Incredible, really, to find that her first meeting with Rupert after the holiday he'd ruined should show her there could be worse ahead. She had to turn her back on him. No argument.

But of course the argument went on. Saturday morning, no hurry, too much time to think. Meg brewed coffee in her smart little pink and green kitchen, staring out across the estuary in the morning light, and saw only Rupert's dark angularity.

She poured a second mug of coffee, took out her pink and green pottery bowl for muesli, and then, after a moment, put it back on the shelf. She wasn't hungry. She'd had a huge meal last night, so it didn't matter if she skipped breakfast. It was nothing whatever to do with being miserable about Rupert.

The cure for a broken heart was work.

The cottage had been empty for over three weeks, and it was dusty and neglected; she needed to Hoover and dust throughout. After that she'd better go to the town and get some food in. A busy morning. She'd make a list.

When she'd done the housework she did actually feel much better. Her long, narrow living-room — two rooms made into one by the previous owner — looked welcoming, filled with light from the estuary. With windows on two sides, it was a sunny, friendly place.

Most of her furniture had been picked up cheaply—the mortgage had taken a big chunk of her earnings—from second-hand shops or sales at Pine World and Habitat. She had two small sofas either side of the fireplace, covered in soft candy-coloured stripes, a material also used for curtains. There was a low coffee-table from Pine World, and a round pedestal table with four wheelback chairs from the same shop in the window near the kichen. She had pine bookshelves, a battered oak chest she'd picked up in Halchester and stripped herself, where the flowers from the ward now stood, in the big pink and green pottery jug that—oh, hell—Rupert had bought her one day in the market.

Until she'd begun nursing, Meg had done little more than camp in a corner of her father's university lodgings, and she had almost nothing from her old home here, only, over the fireplace, the winter landscape of hills and trees and a small lost farmhouse that she'd always loved, and that she'd extracted from her father—who, immersed in his texts and his footnotes on footnotes, never noticed what hung on his walls—

Never noticed anything, for that matter, and certainly not his only daughter, until his unprecedented gesture during this altogether extraordinary holiday, when he had apparently seen her for the first time as an adult human being with a mortgage, and without warning paid this incredible sum into her bank account. He had a good income, of course, and very little to spend it on, but it hadn't occurred to him before to hand any of it over to her, and she'd been uneasy about accepting it. Since she'd left school, she had paid her own way, and she was used to her independence.

He'd looked so shattered, and so guilty, too, when she'd pointed this out that she had hastily swallowed her pride and thanked him, like a dutiful, biddable daughter. Then she'd gone out and bought the new car, driven it back and shown him. He'd been as pleased as a child to see his gesture appreciated.

She needed to get into the super new car this instant and drive into Halchester, or there'd be nothing left worth having in the shops.

She'd fetched her anorak, the big orange canvas bag she used for shopping, her sling bag and her car keys and was making for the front door when the telephone rang.

Her heart lurched. Rupert?

But the caller was Jean, inviting Meg for dinner the following evening. 'We wanted to invite Jon, because he's been so kind, staying on the wagon himself and chauffeuring us hither and thither. But neither of us exactly feels up to a big dinner party, so we thought if you could come we'd be a cosy foursome. I do hope you're free.'

'I am, and I'd love to come,' Meg told her. 'But Jean, do you really want to lay on dinner at all, even for four? Why don't you both come to me, and Jon too? I'm sure he doesn't think you owe him an instant dinner this weekend.' What could she be doing, speaking on behalf of Jon like this? 'And I'd love to have you. I'm just off to the shops, to restock fridge and freezer. It would be much more fun to get food in for the four of us.'

'That's sweet of you, Meg, though it wasn't what I had in mind when I rang you. But I must admit it would be awfully nice just to put our feet up — both of us have had a really great time this week, but it has left us a bit the worse for wear. Angus is much more exhausted than I am, of course, because he's had the strain of his final rounds and his last list, and he's been the one who's had to stand up and make speeches, and all of them entirely different.'

This chat was concealing fast thinking on Jean's part. She guessed that Meg's first weekend at home without Rupert was likely to be lonely, which was why she'd invited her. But it might be even better for Meg to shop and prepare for a dinner party. 'It would be super to come to you, Meg, if we may. Thanks for the thought. We'll be there if you'll have us.'

'Delighted to. Will you ring Jon or shall I?

'Oh, you explain to him, my dear. I'm opting out, as you suggest, and right this minute.'

'See you tomorrow, then. Around seven, say?'

'We'll be with you — on the dot, no doubt. You know Angus. And thanks so much.'

Meg put the telephone down, and her mind hurtled — exactly as Jean had foreseen it would — into top gear.

Off to the supermarket to complete the shopping and then home. Oh, yes, ring Jon. The idea cheered her. In the old days talking to Jon had always given her a lift, and she was pleased to find it still did. It was going to be great to have him back in her life.

Of course he was bound to have acquired a wife and family by now. She couldn't expect much of his time away from the hospital. Probably he had umpteen children.

If so, where were they? And what was he doing staying by himself at Long Barn?

Very likely he had a house in the Midlands to sell, and children at schools there, so that a move would take time. She must ask him about it. She wondered if he'd finally married that actress he'd been so heavily involved with. Tomorrow, maybe, she'd find out.

She called him at Long Barn, and told him about the revised arrangements for Sunday evening.

'Sure, thanks very much, Meg, that'll be great. I'll bring a bottle — what would you like? Have you decided what we'll be eating?'

'Spiced gammon, with apple sauce and jacket potatoes.'

'I can hardly wait. Red wine, then, do you think? I can offer to drive Angus and Jean again, so he can go ahead and have as much wine as he wants. Do him good. This last week has taken it out of him.'

'It's the stress of leaving the hospital behind, of handing over, if you ask me,' said Meg. 'And the speeches — Jean told me that had been a strain for him.'

'We must pamper the old boy a bit.'

'Let's do that,' Meg agreed.

'Now that's settled, how about having lunch with me first?'

'I'd love that. Only thing is, I'll have to be back here fairly smartly to see to the meal, if you wouldn't mind.'

'Mind? Me? Spiced gammon and so on? You won't find me raising any difficulties about you getting on with that. *Au contraire*. How about a good walk earlyish, and then we can eat early too. That suit?'

'Sure. Thanks so much.' Meg put the telephone

down, feeling more cheerful than she had for weeks. Stashing away her provisions in a kitchen bright with the low sun of late afternoon, she hummed a little tune. Life wasn't so bad after all.

CHAPTER FOUR

SUNDAY dawned bright but chilly. Meg bounced out of bed, showered, put on newly-washed jeans, a favourite white shirt of embroidered cotton, and a pale blue cashmere sweater that had been an extravagant holiday buy intended—though at the time it had signally failed in this—to cheer herself up.

Today she needed no cheering up. She was preoccupied with the small jobs she had to fit in, satisfied with her appearance—a ludicrously rare event for a girl blessed with her dark loveliness—and looking forward to her breakfast with zest.

She squeezed half a dozen oranges in her juicer, drank a glass herself and put the rest on one side for the spiced gammon. While the coffee brewed she changed the water in which she'd left the gammon soaking and returned it to the larder; her cottage might be small, even pokey and old-fashioned to some eyes—Rupert's, in fact—but her little galley kitchen had that rare addition, a walk-in larder with marble shelves that stayed cool even in a heatwave. While there she checked over the rack of fruit and vegetables she'd bought yesterday, then returned to drink her coffee and eat toast and honey from the downland bees.

The pink chrysanthemums she'd bought in the market were still standing in a jug in the kitchen, adding a hint of acridity to the aroma of coffee and orange juice filling the air. She'd do the table decoration first, she decided. The rest could easily wait until she came back in the afternoon. If she used her flat pink and green pottery dish for the flowers, though, she'd have to find something else for the gammon. One of the large dinner plates would do, and the baked potatoes could go in a wicker basket.

Right, out into the garden for some trailing ivy.

The air was fresh, the wind from the sea chilling. Autumn was here. Walking over the marshes to the harbour would be exhilarating. And Jon the perfect companion.

Meg caught her breath. She'd had the thought with no warning, and it unsettled her. Surely as far as she was concerned there could be only one perfect companion?

She tugged at some ivy, cut it with the secateurs, and told herself crisply that there was no comparison whatever to be made between Jon and Rupert. Jon had always been different from anyone else, and he had always been the perfect companion too. Nothing to do with love or passion — or brief tempestuous affairs with attractive philandering surgeons.

A slanting early sun glinted off the river as it swept on towards the estuary and the open sea, and she laughed aloud. At herself. Genuinely, for the first time in weeks. Here she was, and life could still be fun. Without Rupert. And with Jon.

A car roared up, and stopped with a screech of tyres at her garden gate. She could hardly believe her eyes. The sight she had dreamed of all these long weeks — Rupert arriving here at Ferry Cottages! He waved breezily at her, eased himself out of the car, slammed the door, and stepped across the paving to her gate. He was smiling, and his eyes were seeking hers.

Meg braced herself for whatever might come, her head and her heart at war again. The natural thing would be to hurl herself into his arms and forget the past.

However, she was booked to go to lunch at the harbour with Jon, and no way could she let him down.

Rupert's eyes had swivelled. He was no longer looking at her. He was staring at the gleaming new Sirocco.

'That *is* your car, then,' he said accusingly. 'I saw it in the car park, but I just thought someone had snaffled your place while you were on holiday. But they hadn't. It's yours.' He was glaring at her.

What on earth could be wrong with that? 'It's mine,' she agreed, and a little demon within her, over whom she had no control, added, 'Any reason why not?' with distinct and unmistakable tartness.

'No, of course not. But how on earth could you afford it?'

He sounded, she thought, thoroughly cross about it, not unlike a husband of twenty years, as if she'd blown the savings meant for a second bathroom on a powerful car for herself. The urge to hurl herself into his arms had vanished without trace, and all she wanted to do now was snap his head off. What had it got to do with him whether she could afford it or not? He stood there, elegant as ever in one of his lightweight casual suits — hardly designed for a cold riverside garden on an autumn morning, more for centrally heated bars in luxury hotels—and instead of wanting to fall into his arms she wanted to slap him.

'My father gave it to me,' she told him snappishly.

'Your *father*?' Rupert was bewildered. Meg had never given the slightest hint that she possessed a father who could go round handing out cars whenever he felt like it. 'He won the pools or something?'

'Nothing like that. All it was, was that he suddenly woke up to the fact that I'm his only daughter—his only relative, come to that—and on a tight budget. So he did something about it, and I splashed out on the car.'

Rupert eyed her as if she'd grown two heads, then he summoned up a cheerful, friendly grin. 'Good for you, Megsie.'

The grin almost undid her, but she'd never cared for being addressed as Megsie, however much it might signify the special relationship between them that she treasured. Today, she considered he'd a nerve to imagine they could all at once switch themselves back to where they'd been before the break and before Sally.

He put a friendly arm round her shoulders, and she knew that only yesterday she'd been aching for him to do just this. Today, however, seemed to be different. Today she had an impulse to twitch herself away, to run indoors and start arranging her flowers. Who did he think he was, to pick her up and put her down as the mood took him?

'Look, love,' Rupert began, 'what I came to say was, how about coming out and having lunch somewhere? We could drive down to the harbour, say, and go to the pub there for a snack. How about it? Ages since we've had a chance to talk.'

Ages indeed! Meg didn't know what had happened to her, but all she felt was a deep thankfulness that she could truthfully turn him down, that she had no struggle over how to respond, because it was already decided for her.

'Thanks so much,' she said, 'but no. I'm booked for lunch, I'm afraid.' Afraid was emphatically not the word. Glad would have been nearer the truth. Or delighted, even.

His face dropped. He was put out, she was pleased to see, and she was tempted to add, Why not put your skates on, get back to Halchester fast, and maybe Sally will still be free? Only pride prevented her. It would look as though she was eaten up with jealousy. Perhaps she was. She really had no idea what her motives were for the way she was behaving, except that they had nothing to do with misery or pain.

'Can't you get out of it?' he was asking.

Why should she? Who did he think he was? Well, that was easy. The answer to every maiden's prayer. And it was she, as well as half a hundred others, who'd led him to assume this. It wasn't just his natural egotism, it was the way she had treated him, all through those magical summer months.

Not any more, though.

'Sorry, I'm afraid that's not on,' she said with phoney regret, and then despised herself for her insincerity. 'Anyway, I don't want to.'

'Come on, Megsie love, don't be like this.' Rupert squeezed her angry shoulders and then patted her, as if she were a child in a tantrum. His next words bore out this impression. 'I know I've behaved like a louse, but forgive and forget, eh? Don't keep on holding that holiday against me.'

'I'm not,' she said untruthfully. 'It's quite simple. I'm already booked for lunch, as I've just said, and I'm not cancelling it. I don't break dates, especially not at the last moment, just because something else comes up. I never have and I never will.'

He shrugged. 'So be it,' he said wryly. 'That puts me in my place, doesn't it? Well, I can understand how you feel. *Mea culpa.* My own fault entirely.'

'Rupert, it's absolutely nothing whatever to do with anything you may have done.' She was beginning to believe this herself. 'It's simply that I don't back out of arrangements at the last minute, and I'm not going to start now.'

'Sure.' He patted her again. 'Nothing to get het up about. I accept it. I'm sorry, but I understand and I accept it.' He didn't, however, believe it. 'Give us a coffee, sweetie, eh? And then I'll be on my way, tail between my legs.'

He was trying to put her in the wrong again. And she wasn't. However, she'd better take him in and give him the coffee he was after. It would be hopelessly unfriendly not to.

'Coffee it is, then,' she agreed cheerfully. 'Come on in; I'll brew up.'

He followed her through into the sunny kitchen. She wasn't going to have him putting his arm round her again, and she gestured at the living-room. 'Find a seat, won't you?' She turned her back on him, dumped the ivy on the draining-board, and the secateurs too, and ran the tap. After this she clattered coffee beans into the grinder and then ran it.

The coffee finally made, she crashed two of the pink and green mugs down on to the counter-top. 'Want a biscuit or anything?' Hardly a pressing invitation, but then he'd barged his way in, hadn't he?

He gave her an odd, almost bewildered look. This was not a Meg he had encountered before. Nor, in fact, had she herself.

'Just coffee will be fine, thanks, sweetie.'

He was perched, she saw, on the arm of her sofa, one leg crossed, his spare, elegant figure angular and almost as fascinating as ever, she realised with alarm.

She plonked a coffee-mug on the table. 'Carry on, won't you?' she invited. 'I'm going to get on with arranging the flowers, because I've got the Hendersons coming for dinner tonight, and I want to have the flowers done before I go out.'

Suddenly Meg seemed to be moving in exalted circles! Rupert was about to cross-examine her when a car drew up outside, without any screech of tyres this time. Both of them recognised Jon's white Audi. Rupert's jaw dropped, and he began reassembling his ideas.

Meg's face, though of this she was totally unaware, lit up. Her troubles were over. Jon was here. Rupert would stop putting pressure on her. Her hands full of chrysanthemums, she flew to her front door and had it open as Jon came up the path.

'Hi,' she said, radiant. 'Great to see you.'

The joy in her voice jolted Rupert, and gave his spinning mind yet another problem to assimilate.

'I'm just doing the flowers for tonight,' she went on. 'Rupert's here — he looked in for coffee — but he's practically on his way.'

Jon looked interested, which he was. He'd guessed the car to be Rupert's, and had come up the path wondering if he was expected to bow gracefully out of the walk over the marshes and their lunch together. Meg's words, though, appeared to be a clear signal to do no such thing, and he was more than ready to play it her way.

'I'd love a coffee,' he said. 'Thanks.' He followed her in, nodded to a tense and wary-looking Rupert. 'Morning.' He sniffed appreciatively. 'Smells delicious in here. What is it, as well as the coffee? I know — oranges. Right?'

Meg's eyes were gleaming. 'Right,' she agreed, laughter and happiness in her voice. Suddenly she was relaxed and happy. Everything was going to be all right. 'Oranges for the spiced gammon. Oranges and cinnamon go into it,' she explained.

'I knew this was going to be a meal to remember,' Jon told her, as he saw Rupert staring angrily into his coffee.

Meg was pouring coffee for Jon. 'You take that,' she told him, 'and I'll get on with the flowers, so we can be off for our walk. Super day for it.'

'Should be,' Jon agreed. Long-legged in jeans and a cream fisherman's sweater, he strolled through to the living-room and scrutinised the beginning of her flower arrangement — trailing ivy in the pottery dish and, so far, a mere scattering of pink chrysanthemum heads.

'This is going to look really good,' he said. 'I like this dish.'

Rupert saw his opportunity, and he took it. 'Meg and I picked it up in Halchester market,' he informed Jon, challenge in his eyes and the set of his head as well as in his voice. Hands off my woman, he was announcing.

He went on announcing it, too, until Meg began to feel like a parcel of land, disputed territory, laid claim to by a couple of pushy lords of the manor. She was amused. Highly sceptical too. She didn't believe either of them was in fact involved with her at this point. Only with each other.

Since Rupert showed no sign of departing, she had in the end more or less to push him out of the house. She could hardly believe she was not only doing this, but longing for him to hurry up and go.

At last she locked her front door, waved Rupert a cheerful and relieved goodbye, and strode off with Jon towards the river. Behind them they heard the roar of Rupert's engine revving furiously and a squeal of tyres.

'Presumably he's away,' Meg commented. Nothing would have induced her to turn round to make sure.

'Presumably.' Jon's tone was ironic, though his mind was racing.

'I'm sorry he was so tiresome. He's not usually like that — I can't think what got into him.'

'Oh, I can. He's fairly easy to read, in my opinion. Very competitive. He was making it crystal-clear to me that you're his property and I was trespassing.' Jon glanced sideways to assess how Meg took this.

'Oh, I know that's what he meant,' she agreed at once, with the endearing little chuckle he'd remembered from years ago. 'But why, all of a sudden? That's what I ask myself. A month ago he couldn't wait to be shot of me. As a matter of fact, I was fairly upset about it.'

From Meg, Jon recognised at once, this was a huge admission, and he found himself in a quandary. Should he admit he already knew about it? He could land himself in deep water if he pretended not to know a thing, but on the other hand she might be totally thrown to discover that he had heard about it from others in the course of his first week at St Mark's.

He and Meg had always been truthful with one another. He decided to come clean. 'I heard something about it,' he said gently. 'And on Friday evening I saw for myself that you were upset after you'd talked to him.'

Had that been only on Friday? It seemed in another life. This morning she hadn't cared whether Rupert stayed or went, and she certainly hadn't half wanted, as she had on Friday, to stay with him at whatever price and somehow get back on the old footing. She seemed — and about time too — to have regained her sense of proportion about Rupert.

It was only then that she took in the real meaning of what Jon had just said. 'Was I perfectly awful on Friday? You're right, I was upset. I — I would have given anything to have been able to stay and sort things out with Rupert, rather than go on to the dinner party. I must have been out of my mind.'

'No, I wouldn't say so. Only loving. He's the one who must have been out of his mind, to let you go in the first place. And clearly he's found that out, and wants to take up where he left off.'

'He was pursuing me this morning, that's for sure,' said Meg. 'I could hardly believe it—he was doing it before you came, and then he was quite blatant about it after you arrived.'

'My guess is that he's realised his mistake and wants you back. So when I turned up he was afraid there was another candidate in the field. That reinforced his determination to get you back, made him really keen.'

'That must have been what happened,' Meg agreed. 'But if he feels like this now, why did he drop me like a hot potato? I spent most of my holiday feeling miserable because we'd broken up, and missing him dreadfully. That was partly how I felt on Friday, when you noticed it. I'm sorry I was so fraught. I must have been appalling company.' How could she have been so atrociously self-centred?

'I was worried about you, because you were so awfully miserable, and there didn't seem to be a thing I could do to help.'

'I didn't mean to inflict my misery on you—I was under the illusion, you see, that I was coping rather well, and no one would have a clue what I was feeling,' said Meg. 'Do you think everyone noticed?'

'I'm sure they didn't,' he said at once. He was far from sure, though. While she'd held her own at the dinner-table, been good company, he'd thought her tense and feverish, and, after all, sitting round that table were half a dozen senior clinicians, unlikely to have been blind to her anguish. But he had been sitting next to her, after all—with any luck the others hadn't picked up the waves of pain that had hit him. 'You were entertaining. Delightful company.' He didn't want her to suppose herself a failure, which she certainly wasn't, and hadn't been. 'It was only that I was sitting next to you, and I picked up the vibes.'

She gave him her sudden radiant smile, and he wanted to hug her. 'You're very good at picking up vibes — always have been. So as you were there and saw it all, and you've been on the receiving end this morning, perhaps you can tell me what I'm going to do.'

'What do you want to do?' Suddenly he was afraid of the answer.

'That's the problem — I don't actually know for sure. I dither and swing about like a weather-vane in a hurricane.'

'Are you actually in a hurricane, love?' His voice was tender, caring, and he longed to cherish her. All he wanted at that moment was to comfort her.

Meg felt as if he had put two strong arms round her, and she was safe. She sighed. 'I'm being incredibly silly, I know. Two days ago, as you saw, all I wanted was to be able to be with Rupert, and today here he is, and all I feel is enormous thankfulness that you're here and I can make my escape with you.'

She paused. There was no one else in the world she could have shared this problem with, but Jon could be trusted to hear her out, however dotty her tale, give her an honest answer, and never divulge a word to anyone else. 'Do you think it could be that I'm trying to punish him for dropping me and taking up with that

Sally of his? Am I throwing away something that matters, simply out of childish pique?'

Jon was so angry that he had a struggle not to shout at her to forget Rupert forever, he was bad news, period. Walk away fast in the opposite direction, he wanted to tell her, let life bring what it would, as long as it wasn't Rupert. He'd be a disastrous partner for Meg, Jon was certain of it.

However, he clenched his teeth, counted to ten, and dealt with what she had in fact asked him. 'It's possible you're punishing him; of course it is. It would be a perfectly natural reaction, and I think he deserves it. But if you want him back, then you'd better forget about him letting you down.' And, he nearly added, you'd better be pretty good about forgetting, because he'll do it again. And again.

'You think he *deserves* it?' Meg queried. 'You mean, you don't think it's all that awful of me to have this urge to take hell out of him?'

'It seems entirely normal to me. He's asked for it. If you plan to take him back, it has to be because there's real love between you, hasn't it? It has to be because there's a relationship that matters, as I see it; it has to be more than a passing affair.'

'But he's never been serious about a woman in his life. What we had was never meant to be more than a temporary affair. He was perfectly honest about that, from the beginning.'

He was, was he? Jon raged to himself. Meg was not the sort of girl to treat lightly, and he wasn't going to stand by passively and watch Rupert make a mess of her emotions. Already he'd hurt her badly. He mustn't be allowed to do it again. Not while he, Jonathan Drew, was around to put a stop to it.

'I don't actually know if he does want us to start up again,' Meg said reflectively. 'He may just be trying to see we're still friends, no hard feelings, that kind of thing.'

'Time will show whether you want to go on with a serious relationship with him, of whatever sort the two of you can work out between you. To be long-term, you'll agree, it has to be something that suits you both.' Jon found the prospect of anything of the kind wholly unappealing. Well, naturally he didn't like it, he told himself. Rupert wasn't half good enough for Meg; that was all there was to it. But if she decided she wanted him back, she should have him. He'd see to that. It would be easy enough.

'It would be easy enough to get him back, you know, if you really want him,' he told her.

She was entirely disbelieving. 'I don't think so—no way. You're joking.'

'No, I'm not. It's the chase he enjoys, and winning, especially if someone else—like me, say—loses. Hard to get is what's important when you're dealing with him; that's fairly obvious. So what you have to do is come out with me a few times, like this morning, and he'll be there fighting to get you back. Count on it.'

Meg wrinkled her nose, sprinkled liberally with freckles from the summer. They'd been walking into the wind off the sea, and she was flushed now, and with her hair blowing off her forehead she looked, Jon decided, magnificent. No wonder Rupert wanted her back—the problem was why he'd ever been fool enough to let her go.

'I see that what you say is very likely true,' she was saying doubtfully. 'But, apart from anything else, that's never been the kind of relationship I've wanted — based on one-upmanship, instead of trust or enduring love. And if that's what I have to do to have Rupert back, I despise myself for wanting to do it, for even thinking of it. That's not the kind of partnership I want for the rest of my life.'

Try despising Rupert, not yourself, Jon longed to tell her. But he didn't. Today was not the right time — far too soon. She was raw with pain. 'Play it like a game, love, why don't you?' he suggested. But could she possibly? 'Take it easy,' he added for good measure. 'My guess is that for the sake of your self-respect you need, to put it at its lowest, to win a round. After that you'll be in a stronger position, and you'll be able to stand back and decide what you truly feel about him. And I'm here ready to partner you for the next round. You have but to say the word.'

Suddenly it did sound like fun. And Rupert had asked for it. What was more, with Jon's help, she'd very likely pull it off.

'You know,' Meg told him, her eyes laughing now, 'you're being life-saving. I think I can handle it your way. And it should work; you're right about that. And if it does, just as you say, I'll have some idea of where I'm going and where I want to be. I'll be out of this silly muddle.'

'Rely on me.' He gave her a quick, friendly hug. 'From now on I'll be in hot pursuit, dating you for every free moment. And you can watch Rupert come pounding after; I'm one hundred per cent sure of that.'

'I hope you're right,' she said, suddenly anxious. What they were proposing all at once struck her as not in the least like a game, but instead a dangerous reality. Highly dangerous. And far too real.

To break away from these alarming thoughts she switched the conversation abruptly — back to the hospital where she felt safe and, on the whole, in control.

'I can't help worrying a bit about that poor girl in the side-ward,' she said. 'So many things could happen this weekend, and — and of course Sister Metcalfe is as capable of seeing to her as I am, but they're often much more short-staffed at the weekend, and she should still be watched carefully, and——'

'She was OK an hour ago, if that relieves your mind,' Jon cut in. 'I was feeling much the same as you, so I popped in on my way here. And so far she's doing fine — no shock, no bleeding. And so far no sign of infection. Her temperature's stable, her pulse steady as a rock. Her blood-pressure's settled down, and her charts are showing more or less the right readings. I think with any luck she'll make it. She's a fit, healthy teenager, and there's no reason why she shouldn't come through.'

Meg turned glowing eyes to him. 'Am I glad to hear you! I've been quite disturbed about her, you know.'

'Well, of course she's got a long, hard haul ahead, but I see no reason why she shouldn't make it, provided, that is, she has the psychological stamina to handle the weeks of immobilisation and discomfort.'

'Certainly that won't be the least of it,' said Meg.

'One thing at a time, love. It's her physical condition we have to worry about this weekend, and, as I say, that does seem to be OK. Worries about her morale come later. Like next week, say,' Jon laughed cheerfully.

It was good to be with him again. A sense of warm security and genuine hopefulness flooded Meg, rather to her surprise. She hadn't felt like this for what seemed a long, long time.

The wind from the sea blew in her face, while a wintry sun shone down from a pale sky on to the wide, glittering estuary spread before them. Meg turned to Jon. 'Isn't this brilliant?'

'Fantastic,' he agreed.

CHAPTER FIVE

THE dinner party was a huge success, and the Hendersons stayed late. Jon drove them home, and then, to Meg's delight, returned to help her with the washing up.

'Maybe now I'm in the money I'll run to that dishwasher I've always been promising myself,' she said.

'In the money, are you?' The dark eyes glinted. 'I had registered that you're fabulously dressed, and running a pricey car, with this year's registration too, but I assumed nursing sisters were at last being paid a respectable salary.'

'The salary is better than it was, but you still have to give up bedside nursing to move into the upper salary ranges,' she told him. 'I've been fairly broke, though, ever since I took on the mortgage for this place. I offset the monthly payments at first by having a lodger — the physio who'd been sharing with the previous owner. But when she left I longed to have the place to myself, and that meant a very tight budget.'

'Had a legacy, then? Or been lucky on the horses?'

'Nothing like that. It's Dad who suddenly stumped up. In fact, come to think of it, if Rupert hadn't let me down over the holiday I'd still be poverty-stricken. I went home, you see, and mooched around feeling sorry for myself.'

'A very natural reaction,' Jon told her, though once

again he simmered inwardly, and thought of a number of horrible torments he would be delighted to inflict on Rupert.

'No, it was incredibly feeble. But I couldn't seem to summon up the energy to do anything else. Anyway, because I was at home, Dad eventually went so far as to notice my clapped-out old heap of a car, and he said wasn't it about time I changed it for a newer model? Was I safe, he demanded, on the roads in it? So I said it was a splendid idea, thanks very much, and what was I supposed to use for money?'

'So what did he say to that? "Here you are, my darling daughter, take this sock full of gold and go buy yourself a nice new car"?'

'That's more or less what he did say. You know how incredibly vague he is, head either in the clouds or in some ancient tome, and he just gaped at me. "Are you short of *cash*, Meg?" he enquired blankly. "Whyever haven't you said?" So I muttered something about always having paid my own way, and that being what I wanted, in fact — which is true. And he did some more gaping, and then said, "Quite right, you always have. I don't suppose I've paid a penny out for you since you left school."'

'Had he not? A bit much, that, I'd say.' Jon frowned. Meg's life did seem to be cluttered with the most useless men. A good thing he'd come back into it, and someone could do some looking out for her.

'It didn't occur to me there was anything odd about it — I suppose I never realised he was anything but a badly paid lecturer,' she said. 'But apparently that was way back. He does have a Chair, after all — and, what's more, he's had it for years and years. I was at school when he suddenly became "the Professor". I thought it was frightfully grand. And Mother remarried when I was ten, and since then he's paid nothing out for her, and since I was eighteen nothing for me either. And he simply doesn't spend, you see. That's what I hadn't understood. His needs are minimal. He has his flat on the campus, and his department secretary who sees to everything, including buying his shirts and organising the daily help. So there's practically nothing going out. He hauled me off to see his accountant, who said he could work something out to make sure I wasn't going to be financially short again.'

'In wordly terms, your father always was an infant in arms; I remember it clearly. So what did this accountant tell you?' asked Jon.

'Basically, that Dad is verging on seriously rich, would you believe? Most of his salary is untouched, and the accountant has been investing it in this and that, which he seems to have been very good at, and then he's been reinvesting the interest, and so on. He was enthusiastic about Dad having some money in bricks and mortar — evidently he's been trying to make him buy property for years. So now Dad's paid off my mortgage, and he owns this house. He won't let me pay a penny for it, it's safely willed to me — with all the rest of his accumulation of funds — and every year from now on he's making me a tax-free gift. This, the accountant swears, is to Dad's advantage. So here I am, suddenly without any financial worries — spend, spend, spend could be my motto entirely safely, as far as I can see.'

'So you bought a new car. And quite right too. And

I agree, you'd better go out and get that dishwasher soonest. Like tomorrow, say? I'll come with you and buy it in the lunch-hour, shall I? I'd like to buy a dishwasher.'

Meg blinked. Jon had always been like this—no sooner said than done. It was one of the reasons why life with him around was lived in the fast lane. It was what she had missed when he'd departed for his next hospital at the other end of the country. Even so, tomorrow?

Today. The kitchen clock told her it was one in the morning.

'See how the day goes, shall we?' she said weakly. 'After all, it's your first day in charge—anything may crop up.'

'Anything may, and no doubt will,' he agreed. 'But, subject to emergencies, let's go and buy a dishwasher in the lunch-hour. We can pick up a sandwich and coffee in Halchester—it'd be fatal to eat in the canteen; we'd be bound to get caught for something or other. And, by the way, you're booked for the evening too. I told Angus we'd drop by and report on how St Mark's is holding up without him.'

'Oh, Jon, what a good idea. Just what he needs.'

'Retirement comes hard to most surgeons. Even when you know your reaction times are slowing up, and standing for hours in a hot theatre doesn't suit you as it used to, it's hard to lose a way of life that's been with you since you qualified. Anyway, they're giving us sherry. They would have provided a complete meal, but I told them I was taking you out—shall I book a table at Long Barn, or would you rather go further afield this time?'

'Long Barn will be fine,' Meg said faintly.

'Good. We'll have plenty of time during the evening to plan enough interesting outings to send Rupert right round the twist,' Jon told her with satisfaction. 'Don't forget to make sure he knows you're booked up tomorrow, will you?'

Wiping down the sink, Meg chuckled. 'I'll do that. And thanks for helping me with the washing up, and for the rest of today. It's been great.' She stretched up and kissed him happily on the cheek, as she'd done when she was younger, and only after he'd hugged her and departed did it occur to her to wonder what on earth she could have been thinking of.

She was too tired to work it out, though, and fell asleep the moment she turned her light out, waking to the imperative bleeping of her alarm at six-thirty. She stretched, and sprang out of bed, eager for the day ahead.

This morning, as she sped along the corridors towards the ward, Meg wasn't even faintly conscious of Rupert, or indeed of any personal problems. She wanted to see the patient in the side-ward, hoping she would be as much improved as Jon had found her yesterday, and planning how she'd arrange to have her looked after adequately—she knew she was hardly likely to be offered any extra staff this week.

As she turned into the ward, she glimpsed a white-coated figure going into the side-ward. Duncan. She followed hard on his heels, and discovered Jon and Drip-Dry already in there, with Rebecca.

'Morning,' Meg said briskly to all and sundry.

Jon looked up. 'Hi. Bang on cue — we're having an early case conference. Janey's come along nicely, hasn't she?'

'Much, much better than when I last saw her,' Meg agreed, with huge enthusiasm directed at the patient herself. All right, so Janey was enormously improved, and certainly, in that age-old phrase, 'doing better than expected' or, indeed, feared. But she was a pale wisp of a girl, dominated by the batteries of apparatus attached to her pathetically frail and vulnerable frame. Some of the tubes and drips in place on Friday were no longer needed, and had been removed, but her abdominal wound still required drainage, and her fractured leg, of course, would have to remain immobilised in the external fixator Jon had screwed into it in the theatre.

This fixator, doing its own particular job of maintaining the correct alignment of Janey's broken bones, seemed to the unprofessional eye a cumbersome piece of engineering with its array of what were rather misleadingly termed pins, in fact metal bars and screws. It allowed skin wounds to be regularly dressed and then to heal by exposure to the air. It was therapeutic, but it remained an awkward and heavy piece of metalwork, which would catch on bedclothes if Janey moved incautiously. Hitting its pins would hurt her.

As they'd been saying yesterday, Janey had a long, hard road ahead of her, and she looked such a child. The notes gave her age as seventeen, but just now she looked more like fourteen. A child who needed her mother.

And where was that mother? Still sitting with the

badly injured father? Meg made a mental note to get on to Intensive Care and find out.

Janey's eyes were huge and trusting in her wan face as she hung on Jon's every word. Meg knew how she felt. He was giving it to her, straight from the shoulder.

'It's not going to be easy for you; I can't pretend it is. You're going to have to work hard at getting better. How well you do depends mainly on you. We're all going to keep on making demands on you, we're going to ask you to move about and exercise when it still hurts you, and we're going to expect you to tire yourself out, the moment these drainage tubes are out of your tummy wound, by moving about much more than you'll feel inclined to. This fixator on your leg is a super piece of apparatus, and it's doing a great job for your injured leg, holding your broken bones in place. But it is going to make your leg clumsy and heavy, and quite difficult for you to move. It'll hurt your leg, too, if you catch it — as you're bound to — on the bedclothes.

'The physiotherapist will go on seeing you twice a day, and your recovery is going to depend on doing your exercises, however exhausted you feel. But I do want you to understand that, however awful you feel now, you really are going to be as good as new in a few months, provided you co-operate with us and work at it. We're all going to bully you and harass you to do more and more, and you'll get thoroughly sick of it. But it's the way to get fit and well again, so you must trust us and bear with us. All right?'

Janey gave Jon a wide, delightful smile that utterly transformed her. She nodded seriously. 'Yes,' she said. 'I'll try, I promise, and keep on trying. And thank you.'

'Now I've said my piece,' said Jon. 'It's your turn. Anything you want to ask me?'

Janey started to shake her head, and stopped. 'Well. . .' she began tentatively.

'Yes? Ask away. Never mind if it seems a bit silly or anything. Just ask me.'

'It's just—I was wondering, how's Dad getting on?'

Meg opened her mouth to explain that she would shortly be talking to Intensive Care, and would give Janey an up-to-date report on his condition, but Jon was there before her. 'He's much better than he was. Like you, he's done well over the weekend. But he's got much nastier injuries than you have, so he's still fairly poorly, I'm afraid. Your mother's going home, though, this morning, to get some rest, and this does mean that Mr Ritchie feels your father is out of immediate danger. I expect your mother will come in to see you before she leaves, so you'll be able to hear first-hand from her how he's getting on.'

Instead of looking relieved, as Meg had expected, Jenny looked if possible more anguished, though all she said was, 'Thank you. Thank you. Thank you very much.'

Jon, clearly as puzzled as Meg, stared down at Janey, took her hand between his, and asked gently, 'Is there something else bothering you? Tell me about it.'

But Janey only shook her head a little feverishly. 'No, no, nothing. I just wanted to hear about Dad, that's all, and you've told me.'

'More news as soon as we have it,' Jon told her. 'In the meantime, work away at your breathing exercises—they're important.'

'Oh, I will. Truly I will.' Janey gave him what could only be described as a look of total devotion. 'I'll do exactly what you say,' she promised. 'No matter what.'

'Poor kid,' Jon said briefly, as soon as they were all congregated in the passage outside the closed door. 'Something's troubling her, isn't it? Perhaps it's a boyfriend—see what you can find out from the mother, if she looks in, eh?'

'I'll do that,' Meg agreed.

'How are you going to manage about her care for the next few days? She needs constant monitoring still, and I don't imagine you'll be able to get hold of an extra pair of hands again this week.'

'I'm going to put Brenda on to her. She's very reliable. It'll mean changing everyone around,' Meg added, more for Rebecca's benefit than Jon's, as her face was at once a study in alarm and consternation.

'I'll leave you to it, then. We should be down in Outpatients now—see you later.'

'That's right.' Meg grinned back happily. Presumably Jon was reminding her of their lunch date, and she found she was looking forward to it rather more than was justifiable for a mere dishwasher-buying expedition.

'We'll need to get a move-on,' she said to Rebecca as the trio of white coats disappeared across the landing and turned down the stairs. 'Get Brenda, would you, and we'll work out the changes in patient care before anything else?'

Rebecca, a little tight-lipped, departed, and Meg sighed. Rebecca never liked changes, and particularly not changes involving patient care. She maintained—

and of course she was right — that it upset patients, and that they were entitled to keep the nurse they had come to know, who understood the ins and outs of their condition and their temperament. Meg agreed with her, in fact, but she also had a ward to run, and a duty to newcomers as well as to established patients.

Brenda arrived, with a separate problem. She was prepared to hand over her patients without too much demur, but she was concerned about her own electronic inadequacy. She hated flashing lights and bleeping monitors. Over the years she had accumulated a vast store of bedside experience, and as a clinical nurse she was second to none. But she'd trained in what she described as pre-technology days, was far too panicky to go on courses to update herself, and was apt to lose all confidence when required to cope with an array of what she called electronic wizardry.

She'd be all right once she'd taken stock of the patient and settled in. She always was all right at that stage — it was the idea of technology that upset her rather than the reality. But Meg knew she would need a good fifteen minutes of her packed morning to introduce Brenda to Janey's monitors.

Rebecca, still tight-lipped, went off to inaugurate the changes in ward routine, while Meg took Brenda into the side-ward. However, the physiotherapist had arrived already, so Brenda was able to go into the main ward to explain the changes under way to her patients herself, and hand them over to the second-year and to Rebecca, who were sharing their care.

Meg herself used the break to ring Intensive Care and make enquiries about Janey's parents. Janey's father was poorly but stable, as Jon had said. Her mother had just left to go home, so there was no chance she'd be coming to see Janey that morning.

'She looked a wreck, poor soul, and can you wonder?' said the sister on Intensive Care. 'She's been through the wringer since Thursday—we all thought her husband was booked when we first had him. But he's tough, he's putting up a magnificent fight, and we're starting to ask ourselves if he may not make it after all. He's a survivor, if you ask me.'

'Odd how you can often tell,' remarked Meg.

'Isn't it? Now if it were his wife who'd been damaged, I wouldn't have anything like the same hope. She's been very devoted, and her staying close like this I'm sure has helped him a lot, but I get the impression— oh, I'm being fearfully unfair, and maybe I'm totally wrong—but she seems to me a right wimp. I could easily be mistaken—after all, she's had hell on wheels here. But I had one of our nurses standing by to take her up to you before she left for home. It never occurred to me that she wouldn't be aching to see her daughter before she departed. But she just wilted at the very idea, and said she'd face that problem after she'd had some sleep. *Not* my notion of a devoted mum.'

'We've all been feeling that there's something wrong with our girl Janey, something upsetting her, and we were rather counting on Mum to sort it out for us,' said Meg. 'Looks as if we're out of luck there.'

'Maybe she'll be quite different after a good sleep and a square meal in her own home,' said the sister. 'Not much good you expecting her before this evening, though—she's not likely to get to bed much before midday, after all.'

'That's true. Well, I've got Brenda Thomas looking after Janey, so maybe she'll come up with an answer before Mum gets here. You know how good she can be with patients.'

'I'd pin my hopes on her if I were you—but I'll make sure the late staff understand about the daughter up there with you and expecting a visit from Mum.'

'That'll be a help. Thanks very much.' Meg put the telephone down just as Brenda's head came round the office door.

'Ready when you are,' she announced.

'Come in for a moment.' Meg related the conversation she'd just had. 'So if you can find out what's bothering Janey, we'll all be relieved. And when—or if—her mother shows up, let me know, and anyway see what you think of her, won't you?'

'Will do.' Brenda, as Meg had known she would, already seemed to be more confident about her new assignment, ready to forget any qualms she harboured over electronics in the need to offer psychological support. Meg took her into the side-ward, introduced her to Janey—pink in the face after her exercises—and more lengthily but surprisingly successfully to the monitors.

The morning whizzed by, but Meg succeeded, a little to her surprise, in extricating herself in time to meet Jon. As they walked through the car park together they encountered Rupert, whom Jon blandly informed that they were setting off to purchase a dishwasher for Meg. Rupert's jaw dropped, Meg was delighted to see, and halfway through the afternoon he appeared in the ward, ostensibly to check on Janey's abdominal wound.

'Healing nicely,' Meg told him firmly. 'And she's apyrexial. Pulse normal, BP too. Her appetite's not back to normal, but of course we can't mobilise her, so I'd think that's only to be expected. She's getting some pain and discomfort still, but very little from the abdominal wound now——'

'So I would hope.' Rupert was distinctly frosty.

'But naturally the external fixator for her fractures causes her problems. However, you'll find her greatly improved from when you saw her on Friday, I'm sure. Really, she's doing much better than we'd dared to hope.'

'No need to count your chickens,' he told her snappishly. 'The possibility of infection must never be overlooked. It's essential to remain alert to it.'

Was he trying to tick her off? Or was he genuinely worried? Meg decided to give him the benefit of the doubt. 'Of course we shan't let up on our observations,' she said equably. 'But I do think with any luck she's through the real danger period, don't you? Do you want to go over her? She's asleep, actually, but if you——'

'No, I won't wake her. I'll look in again.'

'Jon's still concerned about chest infection, of course—he's got the physios on double time,' Meg added.

'Naturally chest infection is a major hazard in this case; we're all well aware of that,' said Rupert stiffly.

That's what came of mentioning Jon, Meg thought, amused. She should have known better.

'I can't say that my anxieties are allayed simply because she's managed to come through the weekend fairly satisfactorily,' Rupert continued, sounding, Meg thought, like an aged pundit taking a teaching round twenty years back. 'In my opinion she's going to need a close eye for some while yet. I'll look in again later.' He stalked out of the office.

Meg raised her eyes to the ceiling, then realised what she had done, and was amazed at herself.

Two seconds later she was even more amazed, as Rupert reappeared in the doorway. 'Only me again,' he said affably, in a more normal tone.

Meg couldn't help it; she raised her eyebrows in a distinctly off-putting fashion.

'I can't keep rushing off and never getting a word with you, can I?' he asked.

Easily, she was tempted to reply. She fought the impulse down, and said, with a mere hint of frost, 'Naturally you're busy. As we all are.'

'Tell me,' he said, ignoring this, 'did you get that dishwasher you were after?'

'Yes, as a matter of fact we did.' She heard herself say 'we' rather than 'I', and knew it was an error. Somehow it had slipped out, though — and why not, after all? Jon had helped her to buy it.

Rupert looked put out, but to Meg's surprise he persevered. 'How about a glass of something cold and wet over at the Lamb around sixish?' he asked. The Lamb was the old coaching inn down the road from the hospital main entrance, and a regular haunt for off-duty staff.

'Sorry, I'd have loved to, but I'm afraid I'm booked.'

'*Again*?' The word came out as a snarl.

Meg asked herself what she was gettting into. Was this plot—because that was what is was, neither more nor less than a plot, a devilish plot—that she and Jon had dreamed up so light-heartedly, was it going to backfire? Instead of challenging Rupert into hot pursuit, was she antagonising him forever? And if so, what did this tell her about herself—or about Rupert, for that matter? Uncertain, playing for time, she said, almost apologetically, 'Sherry at the Hendersons',' then despised herself for feebleness.

'Well,' he said, 'if you can't do today, what about tomorrow evening? A meal at Long Barn, say? Could you manage that?'

Meg was staggered to hear him wheedling like this. Good grief, she'd won! Jon had been right. His plot hadn't backfired, it had worked at the speed of light.

'Tomorrow at Long Barn would be lovely,' she agreed in dulcet tones. 'Thanks so much. I'll look forward to that. And now, if you don't mind, I'm due in the ward.' She swished elegantly out of her office, and along the corridor, leaving him standing, her eyes brimming with an amusement that luckily he couldn't see. She was triumphant, there was no disguising it. She ought to be ashamed, but she wasn't. She'd won!

Rupert began to haunt the side-ward, apparently worried out of his mind about Janey and the possibility of wound infection. Unfortunately for him, the entire ward was certain that what he was actually worrying about was Meg and Jon Drew.

CHAPTER SIX

Now it was Tuesday evening, and Meg had to embark on the evening with Rupert at Long Barn. She began firmly, refusing to allow him to collect her from Ferry Cottages, though he protested vigorously. She was adamant. 'I'll meet you at Long Barn,' she repeated.

He had to give in, and she drove herself there, met him for a drink in the bar, and then they were taken to their table.

Here Meg had a bit of luck—though she saw from his expression that Rupert saw it more as a slap in the face. The waitress had served Meg and Jon the previous evening, recognised Meg at once, and welcomed her back like an old friend. They were soon chatting away about what Meg had eaten last night, and what she proposed to have today, while Rupert scowled at a menu on which the dishes—and he was normally very fond of his food, as Meg knew well—seemed to hold no interest whatever. She'd been obliged to explain to him that she and Jon had come on to Long Barn together following their sherry at the Hendersons', and he'd taken it as some sort of affront to his masculine dominance, she saw clearly. Too bad.

However, if he was unsettled, so was she, and hidden behind her cheerful banter with the waitress and all the food talk a quite different theme gripped her. The previous evening with Jon had not been a runaway success. They'd quarrelled about old Mr Black, though Jon hadn't once mentioned this patient to Angus when they had discussed the ward. He'd waited until he and Meg were alone to throw his bombshell.

'Old Mr Black,' he'd said, his eyes on his smoked trout, his hands busy, 'old Mr Black will have to go soonest, you know. He's blocking that bed, and we can't afford that. He's not an acute case. If he can't go home he'll have to go to a geriatric ward. It's the only option. I can't think why Angus let him drift on so long.'

'Because he's a deeply compassionate man,' Meg snapped, her eyes stabbing across the table, her trout abandoned. She was shocked out of her mind. Could this be Jon talking to her?

It undoubtedly was.

So what had happened to the Jon she thought she knew? He would never have contemplated throwing an ailing, frightened old man out, with no preamble, no preparation. Jon was young for a consultant, of course. In his mid-thirties, he couldn't have been more than a year or two older than Rupert, if that. Was this the reason why he had forged ahead in his career? Was it because over the intervening years he had hardened himself into the type of ruthless surgeon who operated fast and well and then threw patients out to fend for themselves, thinking only of his results and the through-put in his wards? Economic success, and devil take the hindmost. Here she'd been, welcoming him back into her life with starry eyes, her beloved friend from way back, who understood everything, the truly caring man. What a naïve idiot she'd been. Here he was, Jon Drew, one day into his new post, and he was talking about throwing old Mr Black to the wolves!

Apparently deeply involved with his trout, he didn't even look up. 'Compassion is a fine quality,' he commented. 'Unfortunately in today's world it's not enough.'

'Not *enough*?' Meg was almost spitting with fury, and hurled her words across the table.

'Afraid not. Need to use the head as well as the heart.' Jon put trout into his mouth, followed by a folded slice of brown bread and butter, and munched away before deigning to continue.

Meg sat fuming, smoke, she trusted, spiralling out of her nostrils.

Jon sipped his hock. 'Of course poor old Mr Black's had a hard time, not to mention a rough deal,' he finally contributed. 'We know that, all of us. Losing a leg in World War Two, and now having to have this hip replacement on the other side — rotten for him. Nothing we can do to alter it, though, is there? And the fact remains, he's blocking a surgical bed, and you know as well as I do what that means. Someone on the waiting list has to go on waiting, instead of having their own hip replacement. And waiting in considerable pain, no getting away from that either. Now, as I see it, it's no way to exercise compassion to decide this one can go on waiting indefinitely while we allow Mr Black to potter about the ward because we're so sorry for him. This is real life we're dealing with, with real people, not a romantic dream. What we have to confront is the more urgent need, not the ideal treatment for Mr Black.'

What he said was correct, and Meg knew it. But he was being far too quick off the mark. Here he was, on his very first day as the orthopaedic consultant, and he'd decided that Mr Black was for discharge stat — never mind where, anywhere, any old geriatric ward somewhere in the region, so long as it was now. 'He's a poor old man who's had a hard enough time as it is,' she protested. 'We can't just boot him out because we need the bed. Angus would never——'

'But he should have done, shouldn't he? One of the signs he was ready for retirement. Getting far too soft-hearted.' Again Jon raised his dark eyes to her, and gave her his sidelong smile. Again she refused to respond.

'It's not funny,' she snapped. 'I don't know how you can sit there and make beastly little jokes about it. It's Mr Black's life. I shouldn't be surprised if a geriatric ward didn't finish him off. Angus knew that — that's why he let him go on occupying the bed, in spite of the waiting list.'

'It's all a question of evaluating priorities, I agree.' Jon had finished his trout, it appeared, and he sat back, presumably ready at last to give his full attention to poor Mr Black, Meg thought.

She was wrong. His eyes were scanning her plate. 'Is there something wrong with your trout?' he enquired. 'If so——'

'No, no, it's fine. Very nice,' she assured him hastily, slammed a portion into her mouth and then asked herself why she'd allowed herself to be panicked. 'There's nothing whatsoever wrong with the trout,' she repeated, swallowing. 'I simply forgot about it because

I'm so thrown by what you're saying about Mr Black.' So there! she added inside her head, and carefully speared more trout, which unfortunately tasted of nothing.

'It can't be new to you,' he pointed out. 'He's been with you for nearly a year. You can't not have noticed.'

'Of course we all knew,' she retorted. 'We also shared the opinion that it would be heartless to discharge him. His daughter lives on the other side of the county, and doesn't want him anyway, and although he wants to go back to his own house in Halchester he's not going to be able to manage there on his own.'

'St Mark's is an acute hospital, not an old people's home.'

'You can't get rid of him just like that, with no warning.' Meg was appalled.

'It wouldn't be without warning if you'd done your job properly. But you and Angus both chickened out. I don't enjoy these decisions any more than you do. The difference is, I can't avoid making them.'

'On your very first day in the job?' she asked nastily. 'You couldn't have waited a week, even?'

'What on earth good would waiting a week be?'

He had a point there. Meg searched a little wildly for an answer, and came up with what seemed to her a scorcher. 'It seems to me that it would have been courteous, at least,' she told him coldly, 'to discuss it with Angus. You said nothing to him this evening, nothing whatever. You only raise it now, when we're alone.'

'I've discussed it at length with Angus,' said Jon. 'As I told you, I don't really understand why he allowed the

problem to drift on for so long, and he doesn't understand it himself either.'

'He — he doesn't?'

'That's what he told me. He said he put it down
partly to increasing decrepitude, and partly to a general
fed-upness with fighting the same old battles over and
over again. It's never pleasant to take decisions like
that, he said, but they do have to be taken. The trouble
is you have to fight the staff as well, and he averred
that he was no longer the match he had been for
embattled sisters.'

Meg felt as if she had been punched in the midriff.
'M-meaning me?' she asked bravely.

'Meaning you.' Jon grinned delightedly.

'I — I'm an embattled sister?'

'That's what the man said. Look, you don't want any
more of that trout, do you? They can take it away and
we'll have the grouse.'

Vacantly, Meg watched her plate going and the
grouse with all its trimmings arrive. So Jon had already
talked to Angus about Mr Black, and Angus agreed
with him. He simply hadn't felt strong enough to carry
out the decision to discharge him. And why not?
Because of her. Because he knew she'd be opposed to
it. Well, so she was, and she had right on her side too,
even if she was the only one, it now seemed, to think it
her job to look out for Mr Black.

'Now we'll talk about something quite different, for
a change,' Jon announced. 'This is putting you off your
food. We can resume our talk about Mr Black in the
ward, on Wednesday after the teaching round, perhaps.
Then everyone can have a go.'

So at least he wasn't proposing to boot the old man out at a day's notice. And if he brought it up after the round she'd have some back-up from the physio, and the social worker too.

'Now let's forget St Mark's for a bit. Tell me something about Halchester. What is there to see and do?'

They couldn't go on quarrelling all through the meal, it would be silly, Meg told herself, and, pushing both her anger and her anxiety about Mr Black to the back of her mind, she set out to be informative about Halchester and its environs.

It was difficult, though. Desolation had engulfed her. She seemed to have found Jon only to lose him again. That he shouldn't be at all the person she had thought was worse than unsettling. It was as if she'd lost something very precious. Something she didn't know how to do without. Gone without a trace.

And tonight she still felt like this. Back here in Long Barn, the pain she had felt yesterday flooded her again, and with the same overwhelming force.

They'd papered over the cracks, that was all. Been civilised, had a pleasant, chatty meal together, and then parted politely. But the certainty Meg had known with Jon in the past, the extraordinary comfort of being with him, had vanished. It had been only a figment of her imagination. Wishful thinking.

She must stop exaggerating. All right, so he'd turned out to have a hard streak, harder than she would have believed possible, and he'd displayed it over a patient who — she had to admit he was right about this — was blocking a bed other patients needed. The night before, she'd lain awake fighting the battle over again in her mind, and she had to accept that what Jon said was correct, however much she hated it. But just because he turned out to have this tough streak when it came to discharging patients it didn't mean that the Jon she had once known had vanished without trace. They were older and more experienced now, both of them, and in a working relationship. They could hardly expect to agree all day and every day.

He was also, she reminded herself, the consultant on her ward. She had better, at any rate, see Mr Black's daughter again, and have a good talk with her about his future. If she hadn't been away for three weeks she would have done this by now—she didn't normally allow as much as a month to go by without seeing patients' relatives. But Mr Black's daughter was difficult to catch, as she visited in the evening only, and that not very often. She had to come when her husband had returned home after work, and she could use his car, otherwise she had a long cross-country journey by bus that took hours each way.

Even so, even allowing for these problems, she was seen infrequently, and certainly didn't have a name in the ward for being a loving daughter. The ward said she'd be glad to forget all about her father, and would probably have done so had it not been for his pension. The ward was very sorry for dear old Mr Black, and thankful for his sake that he had so many Halchester friends, who visited him assiduously, afternoon and evening. Once he'd left Halchester for his daughter's home on the other side of the county, he was going to miss them.

However, he could hardly stay in her ward at St

Mark's forever, simply in order not to lose his old friends. Meg knew this perfectly well, and it was hardly Jon's fault. What to do about old Mr Black was a very real problem, and it hadn't been invented by Jon. Her only complaint, in fact, about Jon's part in it seemed to be that he had raised it too soon after his arrival. What on earth did she suppose she meant by that? That it wasn't for the new boy to get rid of the old patient? That was the politics of the schoolroom — and cast her in the role Jon had alerted her to, that of the embattled sister.

In bed in the early hours of the morning, Meg blushed at the picture. Never mind. It was a ward problem that would have to be solved, one way or another, and meanwhile she and Jon were still friends, weren't they?

Yes, of course they were. He had made that very plain, yesterday evening here at Long Barn. So why did she feel so uneasy again today, as if she'd lost him?

Preoccupied with these churning thoughts, she kept the conversation with Rupert on a brittle, social level, though — her mind elsewhere — she was hardly conscious of it. They might have been strangers sharing a table on an Inter-City train. Rupert's face grew longer and gloomier, though this too Meg failed to notice. But help was at hand, and for her the evening was salvaged.

As they made their way out, there sat Jon Drew, of all welcome sights, eating a late meal at a small table near the door. Rupert would have walked straight past him with no more than a curt nod of recognition, but Meg stopped in her tracks.

'Hello!' she exclaimed. 'You're eating late.' She was

so relieved to encounter him, to be able to talk to him and so make absolutely sure that they were in fact still on speaking terms, that her face lighted up and her body suddenly seemed to be on springs.

She hadn't seen him that day. He had been to the ward that morning, with Duncan, but Meg herself had been at a nursing meeting in the other block, and Rebecca had taken him round.

Apparently unaware of any undercurrents, Jon grinned welcomingly, remarking, 'Long time no see — not since last night, in fact.'

Meg smiled radiantly. Everything was all right — and did he know how to infuriate Rupert, or did he? 'Small world,' she volunteered happily.

Jon, well aware of the waves of irritation emanating from Rupert, decided to try to madden him further. Meg would pick up her cue; he could rely on her for that.

'I was going to ring you,' he told her, 'to let you know I managed to get those tickets. So that's all fixed.'

'Oh, great!' Meg rejoined with every appearance of rapture. 'Super!' What tickets was he talking about? Or could he be making it up, to annoy Rupert? That must be it. He was doing his bit in the campaign of monopolising her time.

'Would you like to eat before or after?' he was enquiring. 'Before might turn out to be rather a rush, I'm afraid.'

'On the other hand, I don't know if I could last out until afterwards,' she said. Whenever that might be. Take a chance. 'How about having some soup and a sandwich at Ferry Cottages first, and then we can decide afterwards what to do, according to how ravenous we are?'

'Good plan. Thanks very much; I go along with that.'

Rupert looked as if he was wondering if he was invisible.

'Around seven at my place, then?' Meg was asking.

'Fine. I'll be there.'

'I look forward to it,' she told him. 'See you.' She set off briskly for the main doors leading to the entrance and the car park. What had that been about? Had Jon made a genuine date with her, or had it been no more than a ploy to challenge Rupert?

Eyes sparking with exhilaration, she walked smartly across to her car, unlocked it and settled herself in the driving seat before Rupert had a chance to go into any clinch he might have been planning. 'That was truly enjoyable.' She beamed at him through the window, and neither of them knew whether she was referring to their meal or the meeting with Jon on the way out. 'Thank you so much. The food here is super, isn't it? I must say I'm beginning to feel quite an expert in it,' she added wickedly, unable to resist needling Rupert just once more.

'So I gather,' he said grumpily. He looked like an angry little boy, Meg thought, and felt a brief pang of guilt. But she turned her back on it, let in the clutch, said, 'Thanks again for a terrific evening,' and drove off.

What on earth had happened to her?

Or, to put it another way, if she felt like this now, why had she spent her entire holiday in such acute misery? Had she got over Rupert, or what? She shook her head. She wasn't going to think about it—or him. She was going to bed, and to sleep, and tomorrow would be another day. With both Rupert and Jon in it, and whatever came up she'd be able to handle.

What came up first was the information that Janey's mother had still not been to visit her daughter.

'Did she see her husband in Intensive Care, do you know?' asked Meg.

Brenda shook her head. 'Sorry, not a clue.'

'I'll ring them. I can find out how her father is, anyway, so at least we'll be able to give her an up-to-date bulletin. Do you think she and her mother have had a row or something?'

'Something's upsetting Janey, but I suspect it's anxiety about her dad,' said Brenda. 'If only her mother would look in, she'd be able to talk to her about it. What can have got into the woman? Even if they'd had a row before the accident, you'd think it would be forgotten after all this.'

'Well, I'll talk to Intensive Care, and see if I can glean anything there,' Meg decided.

Intensive Care informed her, with some acerbity, that they hadn't seen Mrs Barton either. 'Not a sign of her since she left on Monday morning for a kip. Not Monday evening—well, she was exhausted, so we didn't pay too much attention. No sign on Tuesday either, so I rang. I'd thought she would at least want to know how her husband was, anyway.'

'And?' queried Meg.

'I got a neighbour, who said she'd come in to see to things, as Mrs Barton had collapsed, and she'd sent for the family doctor.'

'Oh, dear. Doesn't bode well, does it? But I suppose it could suddenly have hit her, once she got back home.'

'That's right,' the sister agreed. 'So I left a message with the neighbour to say Mr Barton was coming along nicely, though still poorly, and left it at that. If she doesn't appear this morning I'll ring again this afternoon, and if I don't get any joy Mr Ritchie says he'll get on to the GP. The difficulty is we don't want to worry Mr Barton with any suggestion that there may be problems at home, so we can't sound him out about his wife. We just haven't mentioned her, and luckily he hasn't asked.'

'Odd, that, in itself,' remarked Meg. 'You'd expect him to be wondering where she'd got to.'

'He's still sedated, and I'm rather hoping everything's such a fog that he simply doesn't realise how much time has passed. He's stable, praise be, but very poorly, and he could go either way still.'

'Oh, dear. I'll just mention the stable bit to his daughter, then, and hope she doesn't enquire further. She's worried about something, and we don't feel it's herself.'

'Perhaps you can find out more about the mother from her? Or do you think it might be too upsetting?' asked the sister.

'I'll approach with caution, and let you know if I pick anything up that might be useful. All right?'

'Fine. I'll be in touch if anything comes up at our end.'

Meg found the physio with Janey, who'd moved on today from the breathing exercises to trying to touch her toes. With the external fixator in her way, she was finding it difficult and hideously uncomfortable, but she and the physio were persevering. Meg certainly wasn't going to interrupt them, and decided instead to make another attempt to get hold of Cathy Stevens, old Mr Black's daughter. She'd rung several times the previous day, but there'd been no reply. Today, however, she struck lucky, and Cathy answered at once.

'I was wondering whether you'd be coming in to see your father one day this week?' Meg began. 'I do rather need to have a talk with you about his future, because it won't be long now before he's ready to leave here; there's very little we can do for him in the ward now, he doesn't really need nursing care, simply walking practice and to keep up his exercises. He can do that as an outpatient.'

The voice at the other end of the line was clearly not cheered by any of this. 'Oh, dear,' it said, and added dolefully, 'He is better, isn't he? I ought to be glad, I suppose, but the trouble is I'm so dreadfully worried about what's going to happen to him. He can't leave Halchester and all his friends there — he'd be lost, and he'd hate it.'

So that was going to be the line. There was some truth in it too. Whether or not his daughter wanted to be burdened with his care for the rest of his days, Mr Black himself was undoubtedly going to hate leaving Halchester. 'He does have a huge number of friends here, that's quite clear,' Meg said. 'And they're all assiduous in visiting him, I must say.'

'More than I am,' his daughter said frankly. 'But it *is* difficult to get over, you know, and the thing is, he doesn't really care whether I come or not. It's his mates he likes to talk to, from work, and the British Legion, the Conservative Club, his cronies from the pub at the corner. As Mum used to say, he's a man's man, a real chauvinist, and the women in his family are for looking after the home and being ornamental, not for anything serious.'

'The fact remains, he's ready for discharge, and we have to think about it. He can't simply leave here and go back to an empty house,' Meg explained.

'No, of course he can't. I wish I knew what to do. If it were just for a short stay, and then he could go back to his own house, it would be easy. Or if we could afford to pay for a nice nursing home in Halchester. That's what he'd like, a nice nursing home where he could go on seeing all his friends regularly.'

'It would be ideal, I see that,' Meg agreed. Mr Black would probably be much happier in a nursing home too, rather than dumped with an unwilling daughter on the other side of the county. 'But if there isn't any money for it, it has to be a choice between leaving Halchester and coming to you, or going into a chronic ward and then an old people's home.'

'He can't do that,' Cathy said at once. 'Tell you what, Sister, I'll talk to my husband tonight, and see if between us we can come up with anything. If we could only sell his house, everything would be hunkydory. There'd be money for a nursing home, and it would all be straightforward. But he won't hear of it. He's going to leave his house to me; he wants to be able to do that for me and the kids—he's always been a good provider, as they say, and he's determined to leave us a proper nest-egg when he goes, bless the silly old idiot. I'd far rather get rid of the house and use the money to see him comfortable and happy. But he won't hear of it — no way. Might as well talk to myself for all the good it does.'

'You couldn't possibly let it, could you?' suggested Meg.

'Let it? I don't know — we'd never thought about letting.'

'There's always a demand for houses to rent, you see. There are the tourists in the summer, and staff from the hospital all the year round. Houses and flats are in short supply around Halchester.'

'I simply hadn't thought of that,' said Cathy. 'Neither of us had. Gosh, that's quite an idea, Sister. Me and Jim could look into it — Dad might agree to that, he might. We'd tell him it was only temporary, like, until he was ready to go back home himself, even if we know he almost certainly won't ever be able to. Still, you never know for sure, do you?' For the first time Cathy sounded eager, even enthusiastic.

'Could you think about it, then, you and your husband, and come in and have a talk with me one evening fairly soon?' Meg wasn't sure how long she was going to be able to hold Jon off.

But Cathy was keen now, and in almost as much of a hurry as Meg. 'Today's Wednesday, isn't it? I can talk to Jim tonight, and then I dare say we can sound out the letting agents in Halchester tomorrow, so say by Friday we'll have some idea of the chances, and we can try the plan out on Dad, and then let you know how he is about it. Oh, it would be such a relief if we could fix him up happily.'

'You go into the possibilities, then,' Meg agreed. 'And I'll see you here on Friday evening.' She put the telephone down with a feeling of relief herself, mingled with a distinct sense of achievement. If there turned out to be a reasonably likely chance of settling Mr Black into a local nursing home, Jon would surely be prepared to let him occupy his bed in the ward for another week or two, rather than pack him off to a geriatric ward, wouldn't he? Or would he?

Well, later on today she'd find out, that was for sure.

Rebecca stuck her head round the door to ask about the cake for tea after the round. 'Are we going to stick with cherry Genoa, or would sir prefer something else, do you suppose?'

'Help—I haven't the faintest notion. Stay with cherry Genoa this week, shall we? And I'll try to remember to ask what he'd like in future.'

'OK. Anything I can get you while I'm out? A sandwich?' asked Rebecca.

'Oh, yes, please. Almost anything they don't have in the canteen.'

'Last time I got prawn and avocado—expensive, it was, but worth it, just for a change.'

'Sounds great,' said Meg. 'I'll try that, thanks. And a lemon Perrier.'

'Right. On my way.'

Meg made a quick summary of her conversation with Cathy Stevens on old Mr Black's notes, then went into the ward, and discovered Brenda helping out with her old patients while the physio was with Janey. She removed her, and told her about the problem with Janey's mother.

'Oh, lord.' Brenda grimaced. 'That's all we need.'

'Thing is, are we going to tell Janey?' asked Meg.

'Seems a bit hard to land her with problems at home.'

'That's what I feel. Tell you what, you just give her the fairly optimistic bulletin about her father this morning, then we can discuss the state of play with Jon after the ward round, and see what he thinks.'

'Good plan,' said Brenda. 'You could see if he'll let us move Janey into the main ward too. I think she'd be much better with company, and she doesn't really need all the monitoring facilities in the side-ward any longer, does she?'

Meg grinned widely. 'I'm sure you'd be glad to have her off all the electronic wizardry. However, I'll try it out on him. I agree the ward would be a much more cheerful existence for her. Anyway, tell her about her dad for now, and we'll see how it goes this afternoon.'

'Right. Do your best, won't you?'

'You bet.'

They split up, Brenda to the side-ward, while Meg went back into the main ward, throbbing at present with the usual pre-teaching-round atmosphere of incipient hysteria. Nurses were twitchy, patients apprehensive, Drip-Dry pounded back and forth from his office checking up on everything he was supposed to have done—the tests for which he should have had the results; where were they and what did they mean, anyway? And what about the latest X-rays? What did they tell him? What was he going to say about them? And had he spoken to all the relatives he was meant to have seen? What about. . .?

Before the big round, the ward tended to be at panic

stations, and Meg usually looked on herself as a much needed oasis of calm, the quiet centre. Today she knew she was nothing of the sort. She was as much on edge as any of them.

It was Jon, she reminded herself firmly, who was coming to do this round, her dear Jon, kindness and patience personified. Or that was how she used to think of him when she was younger. But perhaps he was kind and patient only with the young and clueless — she'd certainly been that in those far-off days — and entirely different with adults during the working day, and especially different with the staff on the ward where he'd been appointed consultant surgeon.

In fact the round went like a dream. Jon made no attempt whatever to demolish either Drip-Dry or herself — indeed, they both came in for dollops of mild praise and benign encouragement. He was glad to hear Meg had spoken to Mr Black's daughter, and had arranged to see her on Friday. Most useful. He'd be interested to know what she had to say, in due course.

In due course. Meg heaved a deep sigh of thankfulness. They came to little Mrs Mulgrue. Meg had had a word with Jon about her — he'd realised himself, he said at once, that this patient's morale seemed to be at rock bottom, but as her previous admission had been before his arrival at St Mark's he hadn't fully grasped how much she'd changed. 'We'll have to try and do something about that,' he'd said thoughtfully, before they'd gone on to talk about other patients and their problems.

Drip-Dry was presenting Mrs Mulgrue, reporting the

details of her daily care and the results of the routine tests that were carried out.

'Lung function?' Jon queried.

'Well,' Drip-Dry began, 'her FEV in one second is down a bit.' This was the amount Chrissie Mulgrue could breathe out in one second. Drip-Dry gave the comparisons for the past week, he and Duncan and Jon had a conversation about blood gases, acid base, residual vital capacity, alveolar narrowing and other physiological details that they appeared to find fascinating, while the rest of the ward round either struggled hard to keep up with them, or abandoned all effort and studied the opposite wall with blank expressions.

Jon turned to the physiotherapist and enquired about Chrissie Mulgrue's breathing exercises.

'Twice daily,' Joanna Rankin responded briskly. Nearly as tiny as Chrissie Mulgrue, but with shoulder-length blonde hair and piercing blue eyes, she regularly astonished the orthopaedic department by the strength hidden in her small frame and the power of her vocal cords. Now she talked about the regular exercises she'd been doing with Chrissie, but refrained, since she was a kind girl, from adding that the patient wasn't actually trying very hard.

Jon turned back to Drip-Dry. 'Wound healing?'

'Coming along nicely, sir. Stitches, as you know, came out on Monday.' He and Jon examined the wound, while everyone else craned their necks.

'Hmmph!' This response from Jon was recognisably similar, Meg registered, yet subtly different, from the sound Angus used to produce on ward rounds as he assessed progress — or the lack of it.

Jon turned to Joanna Rankin again. 'So what do you think about mobilising her?'

'I was wondering whether we could push it a bit, get her into her corset and start her on her feet tomorrow, or at any rate on Friday, or whether we'd do better to wait until Monday. I could give her more time myself, then, because I'm off this weekend, and although the duty physio will fit her in each day she won't be able to give her the amount of time I could give her on a normal weekday.'

'No, I see that,' Jon agreed. 'On the other hand, the sooner the better, don't you think? If you were to get her up on Friday morning for a brief spell, and then again on Friday afternoon, and arrange with the duty physio to make her an early call on Saturday, I'd say she should be ready to sit up in a chair for her family on Saturday afternoon, with any luck, wouldn't you?'

'Yes, sir, we could certainly go for that. I'll have a word with the weekend staff about it.'

'What does Mrs Mulgrue feel about it, more to the point? How about it? Ready to be mobilised the day after tomorrow?' asked Jon.

Chrissie Mulgrue nodded apathetically. 'I'll try anything that could put an end to this lying flat out forever and ever.'

'If you did well, you know, and you were out of bed and in your chair for your family on Saturday, we could maybe get you a wheelchair for their visit, and you could go off and have a family tea party in the canteen, for a change. How does that strike you?' asked Jon.

Her face did not light up. Her eyes did not blaze with sudden joy at the prospect. 'I suppose it might be less trying for them than having to sit about here round my bed all afternoon,' she said unenthusiastically.

'And then,' Jon went on, 'if that went off all right, and you weren't too exhausted, we might think about letting you go home for the day in the wheelchair on Sunday.'

'*Home*?' He had reached her this time. Now her eyes were blazing. 'On Sunday?' she repeated. 'Me? Go home for the day? Truly?'

Meg gave Jon top marks for patient management. What was more, he'd achieved more in a minute or two than she had in several half-hour sessions.

'We can't promise for sure,' he was warning Chrissie. 'It has to depend on how you go. And that's going to depend a good deal on what shape your muscles are in, how well you've been keeping up with your exercises, you know, as well as how hard—and regularly—you work at them once you're in your corset again and off that bed. Isn't that so, Mrs Rankin?'

'Absolutely.' Joanna underlined it, as Jon had intended her to. 'And if you can prepare from now on by doing your deep-breathing exercises promptly and thoroughly every hour, and your foot and ankle exercises every half-hour if you can manage it, it's going to make all the difference.'

'So let's aim at Saturday afternoon up in a wheelchair and off for a tea party with the family, shall we?' Jon urged her. 'Very good doughnuts they have in the canteen; your children are sure to go for them. After that, provided all goes well, home for the day in a wheelchair on Sunday. What I'll do is, I'll look in and see you on Saturday evening, find out how you're doing, and we'll fix it then. All right?'

'I'll tell my husband,' was all Chrissie answered. But her eyes were alive again, and her wide mouth turned up at the corners. She might have been a different woman from the inert, despairing heap who had barely acknowledged their presence ten minutes ago.

'Remember you've got a lot of hard work ahead if you're going to make it home by Sunday,' Jon told her soberly. 'You'll get plenty of aches and pains limbering up, too. Your muscles won't like it at first, and they'll tell you so. And I'm afraid you must expect to feel a bit queasy when you first sit up. So you'll have plenty to bear with.'

'Oh, I don't mind that,' Chrissie assured him, suddenly vigorous. 'I don't mind anything if it means I'm going to be on the move again at last. After all this time! I can't believe it, not quite. You do mean it?'

'I do mean it. All bad things come to an end, you know, eventually. Only a few days now—plus a lot of hard work, and some aches and pains too. But you're on your way, I promise you.'

Chrissie Mulgrue was the last patient that afternoon, and the ward round adjourned to Meg's office for tea and cherry Genoa.

'Do you think I'm pushing it a bit, Joanna, encouraging Mrs Mulgrue to think she can go home on Sunday?' Jon asked the physiotherapist while Meg was pouring the tea.

'No, sir, I don't,' Joanna said decisively. 'Not at all. And it certainly worked like a charm—I'd say that even if she doesn't actually make it home this Sunday, and I don't see any reason why she shouldn't, the mere anticipation will do her all the good in the world. Already has, in fact.'

'Amazing how we all respond instantly to a nice little carrot on a stick,' Duncan commented, putting down his tea and reaching for the cherry Genoa.

Admissions and discharges were agreed almost without discussion after this, and then Drip-Dry came up with a brilliant inspiration about one of the blood tests and a possible new diagnosis of a bone deficiency condition in a patient who had been worrying them all. Jon congratulated him, and at intervals for the rest of the day Drip-Dry could be spotted grinning away quietly to himself. His self-confidence had clearly received an enormous and, Meg suspected, badly needed boost.

Finally they got down to a wide-ranging discussion about Janey, including the Barton family predicament in general.

'If Mrs B. doesn't surface today again,' Jon said, 'Andrew Ritchie's definitely getting on to the family doctor, to see if he knows what's going on. In the meantime, though, we're left relying on Brenda to go on dispensing TLC, it seems to me.'

Tender loving care was Brenda's speciality, as they all knew, but it interested Meg that Jon had already discovered this.

Duncan was agreeing with him. 'Undoubtedly her forte. She may not be St Mark's greatest brain, but as substitute mum for any patient in need she's unequalled.'

Meg seized her chance. 'So you'll want to hear her

suggestion,' she told them firmly. 'Brenda feels Janey should be moved to the main ward now. There'd be more going on, and she'd quickly make friends — good for her morale, Brenda says.'

'She's right,' Jon said at once. 'And Janey doesn't actually need the side-ward any longer. Right, I agree.'

'And if she could have a bed next to Chrissie Mulgrue,' Joanna put in, 'I could work with the two of them together. It would save me time, and they'd be bound to get competitive, and urge each other on.' Her blue eyes smiled straight into Jon's dark ones, and Meg, to her utter consternation, felt a sharp pang of what could only be jealousy.

Furious with herself, she frowned, looked down at the shambles her desk had become, moved papers about in a fidgety way, and tried to get a grip on herself.

'Problems, Sister?' Jon enquired.

'No, sir, none at all,' she said hastily. 'I'll move people around so that those two end up alongside one another.'

'I'll leave you to work on it, then,' he said, and rose. 'Tell Brenda we're acting on her suggestion, won't you? Good, I think that about wraps it up for this afternoon, thank you, everyone.'

The white coats departed, Joanna went to see Chrissie, and Meg was left brooding over her sudden attack of jealousy, and asking herself what it could mean. She was interrupted by Jon, who had shed his entourage and come back to see her.

'About last night's conversation, Meg, if you remember — '

As if she ever forgot anything that took place

between herself and Jon! 'Yes, I remember,' she said, and smiled brilliantly at him, her jealousy forgotten.

'Well, I'm afraid I don't actually have any tickets for anything—it was all a ploy. But I can easily acquire some, if you'd fix an evening—like tomorrow, say? And tell me what you'd like to do—I'm not yet *au fait* with Halchester's night spots.'

'Why not stick to what we said yesterday, and you come to me for soup and a sandwich, and we can decide on the next step then?' Meg suggested.

'That sounds fine to me. Thanks. I'll be there.' His dark eyes gleamed in the way she'd never been able to forget, and his wide mouth slanted. 'Rupert looked sick as a parrot,' he said with undoubted relish. 'I'd say our campaign is going rather well, wouldn't you?'

'Superbly.' Her eyes laughed back into his. 'I was very uneasy about it at first, but you were absolutely right. He only asked me to Long Barn yesterday because I'd turned him down on Sunday. He asked me for Monday first, and I said I couldn't because of the Hendersons, so then he suggested yesterday instead, and offered Long Barn too. He only ever took me there once before, you know, and then it was for my birthday. So now I'm converted to your theory—though that doesn't mean you have to use up all your evenings escorting me; please don't think that. All you need do is make dates, like last night. We don't actually have to go out together.'

Jon pulled a sad face. 'And there was I imagining the woman might be enjoying my company,' he informed the wall opposite.

'Gosh!' Meg exclaimed, reverting astonishingly to the

schoolgirl he'd once known. 'Of course I do — you must know that. I simply meant you don't have to commit your free time to me, if you've other things to do.'

'I'll tell you what I do have to do, and I'd be immensely grateful if you'd help me with it — that's look for somewhere to live. Could we explore Halchester, instead of getting tickets for anything? And have a meal afterwards?'

'Sure, that'd be fine.'

'I can't loll about in Long Barn forever. Apart from the cost, I'll get fat as a pig.'

Meg surveyed the lean frame topped by the crisp dark hair, and smiled. 'You putting on weight? That'll be the day!'

'I only hope you're right. It's going to be put to the test if I get used to Long Barn food every day.'

'Talking of food,' Meg recollected, 'I'm meant to be finding out what cake you prefer for tea after the round. Today you had Angus's choice, but you're entitled to your own, and Rebecca seems to think I'm fairly negligent not to have found out what it is in time.'

Jon stared blankly at her, and then threw back his head and shouted with laughter. The noise reverberated round the office. 'Now I know I've made it to the top at last,' he finally told her, his shoulders shaking. 'Me choose the cake? Success at last. I've arrived.'

'What is it to be, then, to mark the occasion?'

'Do you know, I haven't the faintest?'

'Oh, come on, you must have,' Meg insisted.

'I honestly don't think I have. What do *you* like?'

'Me?'

'Yes, you. Why not have your choice, for a change?'

'We never have.'

'Be bold. Break with tradition. Why on earth should it have to be the consultant's choice?'

'Don't know,' she shrugged. 'I suppose we wanted to spoil Angus a bit.'

'I'm all for being spoilt, too—especially by you. But not necessarily with fruit cake after the round.' The air between them was suddenly electric.

Meg didn't dare to meet those unnerving dark eyes. She fiddled uselessly with the papers on her desk. What were they getting into?

Jon watched her, his expression inscrutable. Then he shrugged and said, 'I leave it to you. Get whatever you like; I'll be happy to eat it up, you can count on that.' And on a good deal more, he wanted to add. Only he knew it wasn't the moment. Not yet.

He had to give her time.

CHAPTER SEVEN

THE following day, amazingly, Meg and Jon both achieved the considerable feat of leaving on time, and met in the car park on what had luckily turned out to be a sunny autumn evening. Even more useful, they encountered Rupert, coming in as they were going out.

'Hello,' Meg greeted him cheerfully. 'Back to work? Hard luck. We're just off.'

'We're going to drive around Halchester and district, looking for suitable properties,' Jon added devilishly.

Rupert's jaw dropped. 'Properties?' he echoed.

'That's right. Can't stay in Long Barn forever, can I?'

'I — I suppose not.'

'Have a good evening,' Jon said kindly, and walked briskly on.

'That was rather awful of you,' Meg commented.

'But it sure worked,' grinned Jon.

'You have an alarming insight into people's motivations, it seems to me.' Meg paused, and gestured towards the Sirocco, gleaming in the late sun. 'How about we use my car? Then I won't need to give you directions, and I can discourse informatively — I hope — about where we're going.'

'Good plan,' he agreed.

'You'll need to put the seat back, as my last passenger

was Rebecca, and she's rather a different size from you.'

'I'll agree with that observation.' Jon spoke with the academic precision he might have used on a teaching round, his mouth lifting at the corners. The assumed pedantry was an old game, dating from their earliest days together, and Meg loved hearing it again.

She drove out of the car park, and turned towards the city. 'You already know the estuary from Ferry Cottages, and, while there are other riverside hamlets to explore, the atmosphere's not so different. So this evening let's go to the cliffs on the south side. You'll find it's a different world — totally different. Spectacular seas, burnt umber cliffs, and then inland little climbing lanes going up into the downs.'

Ten minutes later they were driving along a steep road with views to north and south that had Jon twisting around in his seat.

'Dramatic, isn't it?' Meg said proprietorially, as though she personally owned Halchester and its environs. 'There are some super houses dotted about, here and in the downs,' she added. What sort of house was he looking for? So far he hadn't said, and for some reason she found it impossible to ask him straight out about his family, if any. She was beginning to suspect, though, that — amazing as it seemed — he had no wife and children in the background. He wasn't secretive or duplicitous, not the sort of man who would lead two lives. If he'd been looking for a home for his growing family he'd have mentioned them, talked about changing schools, asked about education in Halchester. So had he not, after all, married that staggeringly lovely actress?

The possibility was incredible at first, but then exhilarating. All the same, she hoped nothing dreadful had happened to — to — what had she been called? Drusilla, that was it. He'd loved her so much. He'd adored her.

When he was ready, no doubt he'd tell her, Meg told herself firmly. In the meantime here she was, functioning as a blend of guidebook and estate agent. She turned inland, away from the cliffs and up into the downs, nosing the Sirocco up narrow lanes with high banks and higher hedges, autumnal now with old man's beard and scarlet hips. Eventually they reached a high, windy ridge, the flickering lights of Halchester below, and the sea, gleaming darkly. The view was lost again as they dived down into an empty village street, a few cottages, a shop or two, shuttered and silent, a farm and a pub called the Wheatsheaf.

'Care for a drink?' asked Jon. 'It's getting dark; we can't do much more useful exploring. And this looks OK.'

'Well-known for its food, in fact. I've been here several times for a meal,' Meg told him.

With Rupert, no doubt, Jon decided somewhat grimly. Meg was driving into the Wheatsheaf's car park, already well filled, though she managed to find a space. They walked along the lane past the two-storeyed building. It was well cared for, its paint shining white, its window-boxes planted for winter with small conifers, ivy, and clumps of brilliant yellow and blue pansies.

'How about us having dinner here?' Jon suggested. 'Could you spare an evening?'

'Love to.'

'Saturday, if they've a spare table?'

'Super.'

The Wheatsheaf thought it could just about fit in another two on Saturday night, so Jon booked the table, and then they drove back to Ferry Cottages for soup and bread and cheese. While they ate, they pored over the Ordnance Survey map Meg spread out on the table between them, retracing their route and showing Jon the villages they'd passed through.

'I rather think I'm going to have to decide against any of those steep little downland villages,' he said regretfully. 'They're much too likely to be cut off in a hard winter—look at those narrow contour lines. Imagine setting off late at night along a twisting, icy lane whenever I got called out.'

'Right, no high downland villages, no matter how loaded with charm.' Meg paused. Now for it. This was the moment to ask him. 'Jon, what sort of house do you have in mind?' How many rooms, was what she meant, and for whom?

His telephone rang. He sighed. 'Here we go. Jon Drew.'

The caller was Duncan, who wanted Jon for what Meg decided must be some sort of car crash. Jon was listening, saying yes and no, undoubtedly, I agree, and other uninformative monosyllables. Finally he said, 'Right, go ahead, and I'll be with you ASAP. Fifteen minutes at the outside.'

He turned to Meg. 'Sorry, I'll have to be off. Cas and the theatres are going to be flat out—two joy-riding kids in a stolen car crashed into a bus shelter, and then ricocheted across into an oncoming Escort.' He shook his head. 'When will they ever learn? Two dead so far, plus one head and face through the windscreen — no seatbelt, natch — one chest and multiple leg fractures, and that's just for starters. On my way.'

He stood up, made for the door, then stopped in his tracks. 'Oh, lord, triple idiot! The Audi's at St Mark's. I'm so sorry. I ought to have remembered earlier; we could easily have come back via the hospital and picked up the Audi. But now there's nothing for it, I'll have to ask you to turn out again and drive me in.'

Meg had seldom seen him so thrown.

'No problem.' She smiled widely. 'And I certainly owe you a good many lifts to and from St Mark's, so not to worry.'

'I ought to have foreseen this. What a fool! How thoughtless of me. The last thing I intended was that you should have to drive into Halchester at this hour.'

'It's only just after nine, for goodness' sake. Don't fuss, Jon.' Was this her talking to Jon? It was.

'Outrageous of me.'

'Nothing in it.' They were standing together in the porch now, Meg in her anorak. She locked the front door, and they walked down the path. 'What an old chauvinist you turn out to be — you wouldn't think twice about Duncan driving you in, or Drip-Dry.' She unlocked the car. 'Admit it.' She settled herself into the driving seat.

He was fastening his seatbelt, and his dark eyes caught hers across the car with a gleam of wry humour. 'You're right, and I agree it's illogical and no doubt out of date too, but it's how I feel, and I apologise.'

'No apology needed. I enjoy night-driving.'

'Thank you, anyway. All right, I'll change the subject; you've heard enough of this one. I tell you what we haven't so far discussed, and that's houses actually in Halchester itself. What possibilities are there?'

'Some lovely old Georgian terraces round the cathedral, and smaller terraced cottages, too, up charming little alleys,' said Meg.

'I must walk round the city and have a look. You wouldn't like to come with me, would you? One lunch-hour — like tomorrow? Or am I pushing it?'

'Of course not. I'd love to.' And it might have the additional merit of annoying Rupert. If he found out. He'd be bound to find out. Like all hospitals, St Mark's was a hotbed of gossip.

On the other hand, what did it matter any longer about Rupert and any old reaction he might have to anything she chose to do? Thanks to Jon, she was safely over Rupert, caught up, now, in Jon's activities, exactly as she'd been all those years ago, and Rupert was receding further and further into the distance almost hourly. It was difficult to comprehend how she could have been so worked up about him. Compared to Jon, he was a nothing.

This renewed companionship with Jon was a joy in itself, and she wasn't for a moment, she assured herself resolutely, expecting anything more than an old friend-ship renewed. That was all. But that was going to be wonderful.

In the old days, with Jon, there had always been something on the go. Half a dozen things on the go, to be accurate. And Meg had been the one on the spot, the one to be involved and go with him as he tore off in different directions. The glamorous, sophisticated Drusilla had been busily furthering her own career in repertory a hundred miles away, and while they'd talked daily on the telephone — in those days, Jon had spent most of his spare cash on long telephone calls to Drusilla — they'd met only for snatched weekends. Drusilla had been the girl of Jon's dreams, Meg simply the useful partner in his activities. Like now. But then, she reminded herself, being a useful partner to Jon all those years ago had changed the course of her life, and for the better.

'What happened to Drusilla?' she asked. The words popped out, and there was no way of calling them back.

He sighed. 'Like every sort of idiot, I married her.'

He married her. A fierce uncontrollable pain shot through Meg as she turned the Sirocco carefully out into the main road.

'I knew it was mad,' Jon was saying, 'but I went ahead and married her. And of course it didn't work. It was obvious from the beginning it wasn't going to work, and it didn't.'

'But you had to try,' Meg said softly. She understood that well enough.

'That's right.' He sounded a little startled. 'No one else could see that, but you're spot-on. I had to try, in case we could pull it off. But we didn't. It fell apart, as everyone had foreseen.'

They were driving into the car park at St Mark's, and there seemed nothing at all Meg could say or do, though she longed to be able to help. The pain she was feeling was no longer for herself, but for Jon. 'I'm dreadfully sorry,' she said inadequately.

'Water under the bridge,' he said shortly. 'And a highly educative experience, I can tell you. You won't find me rushing to mortgage my future to a shallow mind behind a lovely face. Never again. That's why——' He broke off, and frowned.

'Why what?'

He hesitated. 'Probably I shouldn't say this—it's much too soon. But that's why I'm not sorry about this break between you and Rupert, however hard it's been for you—and I do realise it has. Is. Because marrying him would be as wrong for you as marrying Drusilla was for me. It wouldn't work. You'd be miserable, and it would harm you. Rupert's got a wandering eye, and nothing's going to change that. One thing I do know about marriage—you need mutual trust. But all you'd learn would be never to trust Rupert. He'd never be faithful to you, he's not made like that, any more than Drusilla was. There'd be lies and more lies, and promises never kept, and I know too well what that does to you. In any case, you're worth much more than he can offer. He's a capable surgeon, I'm told, but as a human being he's a superficial lightweight, capable only of letting you down, just as he's already done. You're well rid of him, if you can only see it.'

Meg said nothing. What was there to say?

'Hell, I seem to have shot my big mouth off. Sorry. You don't have to pay any attention—except that I'd rather you did. No denying that. But I paid no attention to all the warnings I had about Drusilla, so why should I expect you to act on what I say about Rupert? But I do hope you will. Stay away from him, if you possibly can. You're far too valuable to waste yourself on that prat.

'Right, I've said it all. Far too much, I'm afraid. But you matter to me, always have, and I hate seeing you walk into disaster. If I can possibly stop you, I will. So now you know. Thanks for the lift. I'll see you in the morning, if you're still speaking to me.' He gave her a quick squeeze round her shoulders, and then he was out of the car, his door slammed behind him, and he was walking away from her across the car park.

He didn't look back. Meg watched him until the hospital swallowed him up, though she hadn't the faintest idea he was cursing himself all the way for a clumsy, insensitive oaf, pushing her not only too far, but far too soon. She was bruised still; she'd been deeply hurt by that rotten Rupert. He had to give her time.

It was hard to stand back, though. He wanted to gather her up, hold her to him, and somehow make everything right for her again.

CHAPTER EIGHT

BOTH accident theatres were in action. The neurologists and a plastic surgeon were in one with the surviving joy-riding teenager, who had bad head and facial injuries, while in the other Bill Stanton, the chest surgeon, with his registrar and house surgeon, dealt with the driver of the oncoming Escort, whose chest had been crushed by the steering-wheel. Bill Stanton and his team were midway along the table, while at its end Duncan and Drip-Dry had begun cleaning up the patient's smashed legs. At his head Nicola Ritchie was the anaesthetist, with perhaps the trickiest job of all — to keep the patient alive throughout this major surgery.

No atmosphere of crisis was apparent, though. The theatre was not pulsing with urgency, drama and excitement. The pace was quiet, if not plodding. Slow and steady was the name of this particular job. It was going to be a long haul, they all knew that. They had hours ahead of them in this overheated, brilliantly lit room — for instance, every wound had to be cleaned meticulously before any repair could begin.

Jon had studied the X-rays, and he knew that, in addition to the fractured tibia and fibula of the patient's left leg, there was massive crushing of the right foot. This was what he was examining now, and he didn't like the look of it. 'I'm not sure we're going to be able to save this foot,' he commented.

Duncan agreed at once. 'That's what I was thinking.'

'You mean, as well as the fractures at your end, you'll be needing to remove the foot?' Bill Stanton enquired, his gloved hands busy at the patient's chest.

'Looks depressingly like it.'

As this unwelcome information was absorbed, there was a faint ripple of tension round the theatre. The news was hardly unexpected, they'd all got eyes in their heads, but put into words like this it at once became an imminent danger instead of a nasty possibility hovering uncertainly ahead in the future. All theatre staff hated amputations — not least Jon himself.

'Any relatives here?' he asked the room at large.

Nicola answered him. 'Not so far,' she said. 'He's Toby Dacre, and he was driving his mother. She was killed instantly. The police are going round to the house to break the news to anyone they find there, but that's as far as it's got.'

'No consent form, then?'

'No, not so far.'

'No signature to cover us,' Bill Stanton put in. 'But Nicola and I decided we had no option but to go ahead, and we've signed up for that on the notes. You'd better add your signature.'

'Will do,' said Jon. 'There's no alternative — we can hardly sit round twiddling our thumbs while the police search for mythical relatives, can we? But I don't like doing an amputation with no consent. Well, I don't like doing an amputation, period. However, no need to cross bridges. It may not come to that, I hope. No history either, I suppose?'

'Not in this hospital — and he does live locally. He was on his way home. We think he's mid-twenties.'

'Blood?'

'Grouped and cross-matched,' said Duncan. 'We've two litres here, more coming. And he had a double shot of penicillin before he came up.'

'Right. Let's hope he'll be with us for long enough for infection to be a problem.'

Duncan's eyes briefly left the fractures and met Jon's. He hadn't previously found his new chief a sarcastic character. He was under strain, he decided, dreading the amputation that lay threateningly ahead.

Jon's next words showed Duncan he'd been right. 'You carry on with the tib and fib, then, Duncan,' he said. 'I'll check on the damage to the circulation to the foot, and the nerve supply.'

The long night wore on, while Duncan cleaned and began to sort out the comminuted fractures of the left leg. On the other side Jon worked on the crushed foot, trying to salvage it for the patient to walk on one day in the dim and distant future. Meanwhile Drip-Dry kept his head and assisted them both, anticipating well and never losing the neat-fingered dexterity that had always been his strong point. Jon was impressed, and told him so, and above his mask Drip-Dry's eyes were shining for quite some time, though he must have been about the only happy human being in that theatre.

It all nearly came to an end when the patient arrested. Bill Stanton brought him back with instant open-heart massage, while Nicola stabilised him with superbly administered drugs and gases. But it was a near thing, and they knew it could happen again. Any moment. Bill Stanton was worried too, he said, about the likelihood of aortic rupture, another disaster that would spell the end for Toby Dacre.

However, the slow hours went by, and the patient remained with them. None of their worst fears was realised. Finally they'd achieved all they could for the present, Nicola took him through to Intensive Care, and everyone relaxed at last. It had been a long, hard night, but they hadn't had a death on the table, and nor had Toby Dacre's foot had to come off.

Bill Stanton followed Nicola to Intensive Care. 'You pack it in for now,' he suggested to Jon. 'I can see the father.' Mr Dacre senior had arrived in the small hours, to be greeted with the news that his wife had died, and his only son was critical in the operating theatre. 'Our lad may still not last the night, and I'd better be the one to break that to him,' the chest surgeon pointed out. 'After all, if he goes it'll be from his heart or circulation. I can tell him about the arrest on the table, and that may serve to prepare him for whatever comes — though you never know, praise be. It's still possible he'll be with us for another twenty-four hours, but I'm afraid I rather doubt it.'

Jon nodded. 'So do I. In fact, I'm surprised we got him this far. And if he does make it, he'll have a rotten time with that foot of his. A great deal of pain, and an unending series of surgical repair jobs. I don't know I've done him any favour by saving it.'

'You had to try. And, blow it, you succeeded,' Bill said bracingly. 'What you need, you know, is a meal. Low blood sugar, that's why you're down. I'll see you at breakfast in the canteen — or are you clearing off for a quick snooze?' It was five in the morning.

'No, I'll stick around here. It's my list this morning, wouldn't you know?' Jon laughed a trifle shortly. 'I'll look in and see how he's going in Intensive Care once I've downed a mug of tea, had a shower, and done a few back exercises. I feel as if I've been hunched over that foot for weeks.'

Bill departed for Intensive Care and the patient's father, and Jon turned to Duncan. 'You go off home, and get in a quick kip.'

'You're the one that needs a break,' Duncan protested. 'After all, I've been having a comparatively easy time doing a couple of rather interesting fractures. You've had the stress and the big problem.'

'And you've a home to go to. It's all one to me whether I breakfast here or at Long Barn. Go and say hello to the family, show them you're still alive and can occasionally be seen around the house.'

'Well, thanks,' Duncan said. 'I'd like that. If you're sure.'

'Absolutely.'

Downing tea with Drip-Dry in the surgeon's restroom, Jon, who normally at this stage was assessing the surgery just past and planning the treatment ahead, found himself all at once longing for Meg. If he'd had her to go home to, he realised, Duncan would have been out of luck. He wouldn't have sent him off home so firmly. He wanted to be with Meg, to see that clear gaze of hers on him while she listened and he told her all about the foot, minute by minute. Had he been right to save it? Over breakfast he could have talked to her about it, and been renewed for the day ahead. Oh, well, fat chance. Press on.

He stretched, sent Drip-Dry off to the residence to perform the action—changing his shirt—that had earned him his nickname, while Jon himself showered, did a few back exercises and limbered up for the day ahead, then went over to Intensive Care. Here he found Nicola, with Toby Dacre on a ventilator. He had not so far gone into shock, nor had his aorta ruptured, nor had he arrested a second time. Warmed blood was being poured into him at what looked like a rate of knots, and altogether he could have been worse. But not much.

Jon congratulated Nicola, went off and had a quick breakfast in the canteen, and then paid his usual early visit to the ward to check on the patients for his list. Then once again he made his way to the theatre—the orthopaedic theatre this time—and began his list.

The day went on forever and ever, it seemed, but by six o'clock Jon had got his second wind, and told himself he was as good as new.

Meg's day started later, but it too went on into the evening, as Cathy and Jim Stevens came, as promised, to see old Mr Black, and while Jim sat with the old man Cathy came into the office to talk to Meg.

'That idea of yours about letting Dad's house was bang-on, Sister.' Cathy was enthusiastic and cheerful, instead of tense and worried, as she'd always been previously. 'The agents say we should have no problem—more likely to be knocked down in the rush. That means Dad'll have enough extra to meet the fees of a good nursing home—it's going to make such a difference, I can't tell you. Jim and I have been at our wits' end, what we should do about Dad. I've left Jim with him now to explain about the new plans—he'll take it better from him, you see. He's real old world, my dad, I'm afraid. Women don't amount to a row of beans, except to look pretty and cook the meals.'

In that case, Cathy must be a disappointment to him, Meg thought reluctantly. Thin and spare, like Mr Black himself, and with the same untidy greying hair, she was no man's pin-up.

'That's how he's always been,' Cathy added. 'He doesn't ever bother to take anything I tell him seriously, just says, "Yes, dear, we'll see," and takes not a blind bit of notice. But if Jim talks to him he weighs it up sensibly, gives it his attention. So I've left them to it.'

'He's like that with the nurses,' Meg agreed. 'He chats them up no end, but he does tend to treat all of us like pretty little dears, without a thought in our tiny heads. It's the only thing that makes him difficult to deal with.'

Cathy nodded eagerly. 'He's always been like that. My mum used to say it was the war that did it. He was away for years—in Crete, and then North Africa, and finally Arnhem. That's when he lost his leg. After that he was in hospital for ages, and when he came home to live Mum said he thought home was the same as the sergeant's mess, a place where he could drop in for meals and to read the paper a bit, before he pushed off to the pub, or the British Legion, or the Rotary. When he was at home, he read the paper, as I said, or maybe watched the news or sport on the telly, but if you wanted to talk to him you had to break in across that, and he'd look at you over the top of his paper, or still watching the box with the other eye, like, and you knew he wasn't paying any attention, though he'd say yes and no.'

Meg was struck by this picture. 'In a way he sounds amazingly like my own father,' she said. 'He was never interested in home life, or anything much apart from his work. At home he was vague and kind of absent. He's still like that. Unless you remind him you exist, you don't.'

'That's how Dad is,' Cathy agreed. 'And it's what's been worrying me, because he's never, ever lived with three kids underfoot, and it seems to me it's a bit late to expect him to start, at almost eighty.' Cathy's words began to rise, and the familiar harassed look returned. 'I tried to explain to the social worker how it would be, but all she said was didn't I think it would be nice for the children and their grandfather to get to know each other properly? Well, no, Sister, I don't. It wouldn't work, that's what, and it's no help to pretend it would. What's more, I don't think it's right, or kind, to expect my dad to give up his own home and get used to living jammed up against a houseful of teenagers.'

Meg was cautious. 'It does seem a bit hard. But I suppose it's possible the social worker has something. He might actually grow close to his grandchildren — and closer to you too, perhaps. Better than a lonely old age.'

'He'd be much more lonely away with us all day than here in Halchester.' For once Cathy sounded sure of herself. 'We're too far off for his friends to visit more than once in a blue moon — after all, most of them are getting on too. And, however much we tried, I don't see Jim managing to drive him here to see them more than once or twice a month, at the outside. But that's not the main problem, even. The real trouble is that he's not used to kids. He wouldn't stand non-stop pop or TV, not to mention computer games, and fights over who's having what on, and yelling and door-banging.'

The Stevens' home life certainly didn't sound any sort of haven, Meg admitted to herself.

'Dad can be very much Sergeant Black, you know,' Cathy went on, 'and he expects to be listened to, and obeyed, come to that. If they got on his wick, he'd wade into them like nobody's business, and it'd be happening all the time. Ours is a three-bedroomed house, Sister, and there's me and Jim in the front room, our daughter studying for her A levels in the little room over the hall, and the boys in the back room. So we'd need to give up the dining-room to Dad, and that's a problem in itself, as we've only the one bathroom and our stairs aren't easy — they're steep and they twist.' She shook her head. 'He's a good man, my dad, and at the end of his days he shouldn't have to come to that.' Her face crumpled.

'I do see it would be difficult for him,' Meg told her. In a minute, she thought, Cathy would be in tears.

'Do you, Sister? That social worker didn't; she thought — it was written all over her face — that I was just a hard, unloving daughter wanting to be shot of my dad in his old age.' Unexpectedly Cathy brightened. 'But when I told her to talk to Dad about it, not me, he soon sent her to the right-about.' She smiled. 'He said he was staying in his own house, and he didn't want any assistance or advice from the social services about how to live. He had his pension and his disability money and his house, and no social worker was going to come poking their nose in.'

Meg grinned. She remembered the occasion well. The social worker had retired confused, while the ward, illogically but understandably, had been triumphant, and distinctly proud of old Mr Black, capable in his old age of putting down the social services good and proper.

There was a knock at the door, and Jim Stevens appeared, beaming happily. Meg's heart lifted. It had worked. Mr Black was going to be all right.

Jim Stevens' first words bore her out. 'He's agreed,' he announced. 'Pleased as Punch to have it settled, too. And what's more, he says his friends know all the nursing homes — some of them already living in them, I suppose, now I come to think of it — and they can soon tell him where there are vacancies. He doesn't seem to think there'll be any waiting list either, though I can't say if he's right about that. But it doesn't matter, does it, Cath? He can come to us temporarily, just for a break. No harm in that, so long as he knows he'll be back here in a week or two.

'Anyway, I've promised to look in mid-week, when his mates have had time to come up with some answers, and meanwhile I'm to go ahead with the agents, he says, and arrange with the bank for a power of attorney, so that I can sign leases and agreements or whatever.' He glanced wryly at his wife. 'I'm afraid it seems to be me that has to have the power of attorney, Cath. He says it's a man's job. I did suggest ——'

'No, that's how Dad is. No good trying to change him.' Cathy looked years younger already.

She adored her father, Meg suddenly realised. It was old Mr Black who couldn't be bothered with her, not the other way round, as they'd been supposing.

Amused and saddened at one and the same moment, Meg said goodbye to both Cathy and Jim.

'See you mid-week, Sister,' they chorused from the door.

'And with any luck we'll have let the house and Dad will have found himself a nursing home before next weekend,' Cathy added, all at once optimism itself.

Meg was free to leave now, but she decided to look in on the ward first, and found Jon there, in theatre overalls, standing talking to an excited-looking Janey, who was nearly at the end of her second day in the main ward.

'Hello!' Jon exclaimed as soon as he saw Meg. 'I didn't expect to see you now. What are you doing around at this hour? You're supposed to work days.'

'I stayed on to see Mr Black's relatives. I'm usually here one evening a week to see visitors who can't get here during the day.'

'Good plan. But I hope you take time off to make up?'

'Usually I do,' said Meg.

'But not invariably. You should, you know. I'm dead against overtime other than for real emergencies. Long hours lower efficiency.'

'Oh, look who's talking!' she laughed. 'Very short, regular working hours you keep. Did you get to bed at all last night?'

The dark eyes glinted. 'Do as I say; no need to do as I do.' He turned back to Janey. 'How about it, then? Feeling up to it?'

'You bet.' Janey was bubbling with anticipation.

'I was telling Janey I'll take her over to see her father in his new ward—he's out of Intensive Care now, and Andrew Ritchie and I decided it might do them both good to have a session together. What I'm proposing is to take her along myself on her bed, drop into the canteen for some food—nothing but coffee and biscuits since breakfast, and that was a long while ago—and then collect her again on my way back. So how about you doing a bit more overtime and coming with me?'

'Of course,' answered Meg.

'Ready, Janey?'

'Absolutely.'

'I'll just explain to Staff Nurse what we're up to,' Meg said. 'I'm sure she wouldn't dream of stopping us if we choose to march out with a bed complete with its occupant, but it might be nice for her to know what's going on.'

'Right, you do that while I clear the decks for action here.'

Rebecca's face lit up when Meg told her. 'Oh, how lovely for her. What a super plan. I do think our new consultant's the tops. This'll cheer Janey up more than anything else could. And what fun—I'll come as far as the lift with you, and give you a hand there.'

They rolled Janey's bed out of the ward to cries of 'good luck' and 'have a nice trip, love', but once they'd left Jon spoke to Janey more seriously. 'You will remember what I said about him looking very different, won't you, Janey? Try not to let it upset you — he really is on the mend, but he's had a rough passage.'

'I'm prepared, Mr Drew, and even if I am upset I shan't let him see it.' She laughed. 'And if he's upset at the sight of me and my extraordinary leg with all its pins, no one'll know that either. It's Mum who gets upset, not me or Dad.'

Illuminating, Meg considered, as she went ahead to prepare the ward for their arrival.

'Mr Barton's all ready,' the staff nurse said at once. 'There he is, where we've cleared the space.' She raised her voice. 'Your daughter's arrived, Mr Barton. Here she is.'

The doors into the ward were fastened back now, and Janey was visible. Meg rejoined her, with the staff nurse, and the entire party proceeded up the length of the ward to loud cries of encouragement from its occupants and their visitors. Janey's bed was swivelled around and positioned alongside her father's, the staff nurse pulled the screen round, and Meg's last sight was of a transfigured Janey holding tightly to Mr Barton's hand.

The staff nurse blinked. 'I could cry with joy,' she said honestly.

'Me too.' Meg's own eyes were misty.

'Highly therapeutic too, you'll see,' Jon told them firmly.

'Ever so good of you to bring her yourself, Mr Drew.' The staff nurse was slightly overwhelmed. 'Mr Ritchie did say she'd be coming, but we didn't actually realise you and Sister would be bringing her. I'm sure if Charge Nurse Kenworthy had known, he'd have been here.'

'No apologies needed. I happened to be around, and so did Sister. I'll be back to collect her in about forty minutes — that should be long enough for the first time. They'll both be exhausted.'

'Any time that suits you, sir. We'll expect you.' The staff nurse was enjoying herself nearly as much as Janey.

Outside in the corridor, Jon turned to Meg. 'That was thoroughly worthwhile, wasn't it? I'm glad it occurred to us.'

'To you, you mean,' Meg said fairly. 'It'll make all the difference to both of them. And you've given Janey a huge boost. It'll do her more good than hours of physiotherapy.'

'Hope so — it's intended to. And now I need food — how about coming with me to eat in the canteen? Or do you want to be off home at last?'

'No, I'm ravenous too. Let's see what the canteen can come up with.'

'What I couldn't do to a mixed grill, loaded with fat and cholesterol, is nobody's business,' sighed Jon. 'Tonight is a chips-with-everything evening, no matter how bad for me.' He collected a plate piled with bacon, sausages, egg and tomatoes, as well as a mammoth serving of chips, two glasses of orange juice and a roll and butter.

Meg, who had been thinking along the lines of quiche and salad, weakened and was lost. With her own plate piled high with chips, surrounded by bacon, egg and tomatoes, she followed Jon to a table in the window overlooking the lights of the surgical block they'd just left.

Jon raised dark eyebrows. 'No sausages?'

'No roll or butter either,' she said austerely. 'Though I am, as you see, having orange juice.'

'Truly abstemious. Practically a slimming diet, if you ask me.'

'Who do you think you're kidding? And what excuse do I have? I haven't been sweating off pounds in the operating theatre, so I've no reason for making a pig of myself.'

'Oh, thanks very much! Now the woman's calling me a fat pig — no, correction, a fat, sweating pig.' His lips quirked.

Meg wondered what it would be like to lean across the table and kiss him. He'd taste of egg and chips, and it would be sheer heaven.

A figure loomed. Rupert.

'Good grief!' he exclaimed, scandalised. 'Two cholesterol-boosting plates — what's got into you?'

'Just hungry,' Meg told him.

'I know you usually do have a good appetite, Meg,' he told her severely, 'but this isn't like you.' He cast a censorious glance at Jon, evidently leading her not only to perdition but also to advanced heart disease at an early age.

'Academic rigour is all very well in its place,' Jon said, 'but I don't believe in hidebound observance of every fashionable precept three hundred and sixty-five days a year.'

Meg, having difficulty in suppressing a fit of uncontrollable giggles, kept her eyes securely on her plate until Rupert, after another disparaging remark or two, announced that he was due in the accident theatre and departed, quite as crossly as he had come.

Meg allowed herself to catch Jon's eye at last, and they both exploded into gales of laughter.

'Oh, it's not fair,' Meg said finally. 'He was absolutely right, everything he said was true, and I'm being impossible.'

'No, you aren't. And, whatever you're being, it's not before time.'

'I hope you're right,' she rejoined. 'Otherwise ——'

'I'm sure I am.' But his eyes, as he assessed her, were in fact uncertain. He shouldn't drive her too hard. Last night had been more than enough. He had to give her time — and not push his luck. For the remainder of the meal he talked about the ward. Meg gave him her news about old Mr Black and the nursing home, and then they talked about Janey.

'It was enlightening what she said about her mother just now, wasn't it?' Meg commented.

'Very. Though I'd heard much the same from Andrew Ritchie. He spoke to the GP, and he said that the mother is the weak link in that family. It's Janey and her father who prop her up, so now both her props are in hospital she's gone to pieces. Immediately after the accident she did splendidly, he said, staying at her husband's bedside night and day until he was out of danger. The GP said he hadn't supposed her capable of it. But now she's collapsed, and taken to her own bed, apparently.'

'It does all rather fit in with things Janey has let fall — she has a job, you know, but she also seems to be the one who does the shopping and gets the evening meal.

Brenda says she's been worrying about whether her mother will be eating properly on her own.'

'That fits too,' Jon agreed. 'The GP said he's sure one of the reasons Mrs Barton has taken to her bed is because there's no one to see to things but herself. If she's in bed, and the doctor calling, the neighbours rally round, you see.'

'Oh, dear, aren't some people impossible?' sighed Meg. 'Poor Janey. And Mr Barton.'

'Not exactly Happy Families, is it? The GP has a theory that a lot of Mrs Barton's attitude is fuelled by anxiety, that she's afraid she won't be able to cope, that she'll let them down. Bed is the safest place, and everyone rushes to support her.'

'Now I feel even more sorry for Janey than I did before.'

'I did too,' Jon agreed. 'All I could think of was to take her to see her father. It's not much, but it's something.'

'And it's obviously going to work too.'

'As far as it goes. However, no way can we re-design the Barton family, only offer a helping hand now and again. And now we'd better go and collect her.'

'Let's do that.' Meg rose at once.

What neither she nor Jon realised was the after-effects of their trip. The story of how the new consultant had come down himself to bring Janey Barton to her father's bedside, and fetched her back too, instead of delegating the job to the porters — who would have fitted it in at a time to suit themselves — and had on each occasion been accompanied by Sister Ashton, whizzed round the grapevine. It gathered colour with every telling, so that when Rupert heard it after leaving the accident theatre it had acquired a new interpretation. The new consultant and Sister Ashton were in the throes of a passionate affair, unable to bear a minute apart.

It was a nasty blow, especially prefaced, as it had been, by his own encounter with them both in the canteen.

CHAPTER NINE

On Saturday morning, about midday, Meg was in her garden, picking the last few roses, when Rupert drew up outside her gate with the usual screech of tyres.

'Hi,' he greeted her, striding across damp autumnal grass and pulling her into his arms before she had a chance to take avoiding action. 'You look great. Smell good too.' He nuzzled her neck.

She extricated herself, kindly but firmly, rather as if he were an importunate ten-year-old.

'I did mean to be in touch earlier,' he told her, 'but I got called to Intensive Care. So I do realise it's fearfully late to suggest it, but any chance of persuading you to come out for lunch?'

'Oh, I'm sorry, Rupert, but I'm expecting Jon Drew any moment.' She didn't exactly sound sorry, she realised. Well, so what? She wasn't.

'How about this evening, then?' Rupert asked hopefully.

'Sorry, I'm eating with Jon.' He was coming over for lunch, bringing the first of the particulars from estate agents. The plan was that they would pick out the possibles and spend the afternoon viewing them, and then in the evening have the meal they'd booked at the Wheatsheaf.

Rupert, far from being offended, as she was expecting, smiled tenderly at her, looked deeply into her eyes, and spoke lovingly. 'I hope you're still going to manage to keep some time for me occasionally, love. We're still close, aren't we, the way we've been?'

'The way we've been'. And they had. Once Meg would have fallen for all this, but not any more. She gave him a cool, assessing stare, and he crumbled in front of her eyes.

'Megsie, you're not just dumping me?' The words spilled out with anguish.

Meg felt terrible, and tried to remind herself that this was how Rupert meant her to feel. He knew what he was doing, no one better, and she wasn't going to fall for it. Never again.

'You can't be going to write me off, after all we've shared?'

He was giving it all he'd got, she thought. But he wasn't going to get round her. Not today.

'I know I let you down appallingly over the holiday; it was awful of me, but——'

'Well, it was,' she interrupted. She'd let him have his say for long enough. 'But that's all in the past,' she added firmly.

'Forgiven and forgotten?' He was wheedling like a naughty child, and his arms came round her again hopefully. Once again she extricated herself.

He protested at once. 'Sweetie, do you have to be so stand-offish? It's not like you.' Velvet brown eyes searched hers in the familiar heart-warming fashion.

Only Meg's heart was not warmed even a little. There was something deliberate about everything Rupert said or did this morning. It was some sort of ploy, and she didn't believe any of it.

'You'd better come inside for a bit,' she said. 'We can't go on standing about in the garden; it's far too chilly. Anyway, I want to put these into water — the last roses. Aren't they lovely? Amazing too. It'll soon be December.' She brandished the three stems of pink rosebuds in his face, so that he had to step back a foot or two.

'Very nice,' he agreed almost submissively. 'And amazing, as you say.' He sniffed appreciatively at one, though in fact, as Meg already knew, there was little scent. 'How about one for my buttonhole, eh?'

Meg smiled inwardly. She should have expected this swift recovery. Slick footwork, that had always been Rupert's trademark. 'They were intended for my dressing-table,' she said repressively. 'But I dare say I can spare you one.' That put him back in his place, she hoped, as she snipped at a stalk and fitted the bud into his buttonhole with hands as steady as a rock. 'You'd better come in and have a drink before you go,' she told him, emphasising 'go' rather more than was kind.

'Thanks, I'd like that,' he said, continuing to smile intimately and lovingly at her.

Meg led the way into her little pink and green kitchen, filled a bud vase, stripped the leaves from the roses and arranged them, putting them on the windowsill above the sink. No way was she going to be daft enough to take them upstairs to her room with Rupert crowding behind her; instead she went briskly towards the pine dresser at the dining end of her long living-room. 'Dry sherry?' One of Rupert's characteristics — unkind people described it as one of his affectations — was this taste for dry sherry, which, in addition, he particularly liked to drink before lunch on Saturday, to mark the onset of civilised weekend habits. It was a sort of young fogeyish attitude which, allied to his sharp suits and brilliantly striped shirts—today's was puce and white—painted a picture that he cherished.

Once Meg had cherished it too. This morning, however, it no longer impressed her, and the tug at her heart that would in the past have come instantly as she saw his lean frame leaning nonchalantly against the edge of her pine table failed to materialise.

She was over him.

Hurrah! She was free. He was nothing in her life. She poured sherry into the heavy modern glasses that she'd picked up for a song at the reject shop, and handed one to Rupert.

He raised it to her, and looked over the rim into her eyes. 'Like old times,' he told her, his words heavy with meaning.

Unwanted meaning. 'Old times?' Meg repeated. 'Hardly. Last summer, for Pete's sake. Not exactly lost in the mists of remembered time.'

'No,' he agreed hastily. 'You're right, of course. No time ago at all.' He studied his sherry glass, turning it round in his capable surgeon's hands that Meg had once loved so agonisingly and now was able to watch dispassionately. She thought he was going to curry yet more favour by admiring it effusively, but she was wrong.

'Since you're so moneyed these days,' he told her cheerfully, 'you could easily afford some decent sherry glasses at last, couldn't you? Waterford, say, or Edinburgh crystal. Something to do justice to this excellent sherry.'

Meg was outraged, but at the same time she found she could read him clearly. He knew perfectly well that she stocked this sherry for him, and the knowledge had gone to his head, restored his waning confidence in his power over her. She gave him a look that seared. 'I like these glasses,' she said firmly. 'And I'm not much enamoured of cut glass.' Nor of you, her tone added.

Quite what would have happened next she was never to discover, as they were interrupted by the telephone. It was Jon, crying off lunch. Detained at Casualty, he told her. Meg's spirits sagged, though at the other end of the telephone this was in no way apparent to Jon. All she said was, 'All right. Never mind. I'll expect you this evening, around six to seven. Or I could meet you at the Wheatsheaf, if that would be any help? No. Right. Between six and seven, then, here. See you.' She put the telephone down.

'Rotten luck.' Rupert oozed what Meg knew had to be false sympathy. He'd be delighted. Things were going his way, and there was nothing much she could do about it. 'However,' he went on, cashing in straight away, as she'd expected him to — no one would ever call Rupert a slow worker — 'however, it's an ill wind — my good fortune. You can come out to lunch with me now, can't you, sweetie? How about the Halchester coffee shop? And then we could stroll round the antique shops in the alleys? You like doing that, and I'll make sure you're back here in plenty of time to get dolled up for this evening.'

He wouldn't, of course. Nothing wrong with his technique ever, and Meg was sure he'd manage to arrange it so that she was late and rushed, throw on the nearest garment to hand, and had no time for more than a quick dab of powder on a shiny nose.

Even so, it seemed unnecessarily brutal to throw him out just before lunch, when here it was, ready and waiting. 'I've been to Halchester once today,' she said, 'and I don't really want to go again. But lunch is all ready here, if you'd like to share it with me. Instead of Jon,' some imp in her mind made her add.

'Sure that's all right? I did mean to take you somewhere, you know.'

'Only baked potato and salad, with some cold ham,' she warned him, thinking this might make him turn her offer down. Saturday lunch was meant to be quite something, one of the landmarks of Rupert's weekend, a suitable follow-up to the dry sherry.

'Sounds great,' he responded eagerly, taking her aback. 'It'll be really super to have a meal with you again in this charming little room with its amazing views.'

Meg didn't believe a word of it. She knew perfectly well that Rupert had never rated her cottage at all highly. It had been reassuring — indeed, a joy — to find that Jon thought it a delight. She gave Rupert a suspicious look. He was flannelling, chatting her up, and lying in his back teeth. How could he? However, since it looked as though they were stuck with lunching together, she'd break through this load of nonsense. It was time they talked straight. Honestly, as they'd once done.

Rupert was continuing with his enthusiastic approval of everything in sight, including the distinctly ordinary food she had placed before him. Over the pink and green pottery, Meg eyed him. Very Rupert, she decided — enormously charming, highly entertaining. He was into his act.

She'd seen it before, of course. They all had. And when she'd first gone out with him, while flattering and huge fun, it had still been something of a lark to have this attention turned fully on to her alone. To find herself the focus for Rupert's act had eventually gone to her head, that had been the trouble. The charm had worked. She had counted on it, and begun to need it. She had, to be honest, grown addicted to Rupert's blend of blandishment and sexy kind of teasing provocation. He hadn't taken it seriously. But she had.

Today, though, this wasn't the whole story. There was something different, not in her, but in him. It wasn't merely that she had regained her immunity. If that had been all, she would have enjoyed his performance. It would have been the same sort of fun it always had been — enhanced, probably, by the fact that he no longer had any power to hurt her.

But today there was something wrong. It wasn't fun for Rupert, she could see that. It wasn't a light-hearted lark. It was a little desperate. Frenzied, even?

She had to be wrong. Rupert, of all people, desperate to get her back? He wasn't like that. For him there would always be a mass of talent waiting in the wings.

The explanation came to her as clearly as if Jon had spoken it into her ear. Rupert was above all competitive. He would hate losing her to anyone else. Hence the desperation. Normally, while he could undoubtedly be truthfully labelled a woman-chaser, he chased with a high degree of skill, and what the world actually perceived was a decorative cast of lovely ladies chasing Rupert.

Now he must be afraid she had dropped him in favour of Jon—who, adding insult to injury, was a consultant, and senior to him. So he was determined to get her back.

Thoughtfully she helped herself to more salad from the big pottery bowl they'd bought together in Halchester market one happy Saturday morning when the world had seemed to be opening up gloriously for them both. As long as you took him lightly, easily, Rupert was marvellous value, and they'd had a terrific summer together.

He had been, she could see it now it was over, very good for her. Very good indeed. He'd given her a confidence she had never possessed before—though he'd ended by destroying it. But while they were together he'd improved her dress sense out of all recognition, he'd introduced her to sophisticated restaurants of which she'd previously known less than nothing, he'd given her days a lift they'd not known before, and she had thrived on it—until, sadly, she hadn't known how to do without it.

That had been her mistake, though, not his. He'd told her at the outset that he couldn't be called the faithful type. How right he'd been. Her trouble was that she almost certainly was exactly that. But not forever. Not where Rupert was concerned, anyway. Those summer days had been essentially ephemeral. It had all been surface fun. No more, no less.

It was nothing to do with Rupert, really, that the attention he'd lavished on her had been addictive. It had, after all, been something totally lacking in her life, and once she experienced it she knew at first hand what she had lacked. It was true she'd always been the unwanted, unneeded child in her broken family, and she'd imagined she'd come to terms with this early in her teens. Evidently she hadn't. But it wasn't Rupert's responsibility to make it up to her — though this was what he had inadvertently done. He had shown her what had been lacking in her life.

'We had a fantastic summer,' she told him. 'I think probably I'll always remember it. I'm immensely grateful for it — you sort of set me up, you know. Made me feel wanted. It was truly great.'

He dropped his knife and fork as if they'd stung him long before she'd finished, and his eyes met hers. No longer velvety, they held shock — alarm, even.

'That sounds hideously final. I hope I'm wrong.'

Thank God he'd stopped pretending.

'You know you're not wrong. As you've said, we'll always be friends, I'm sure,' she said. Only she wasn't. 'But anything more — and it was terrific — belongs to last summer, not to today. You know that as well as I do, so just stop pretending about it, will you?'

'Pretending?' It was an astonished yelp.

'Pretending,' Meg repeated. 'That's what you've been doing ever since you got here, and you know it.'

'If I've been pretending,' he said slowly, 'it's only because I can't tell where I stand with you. I don't seem to be able to reach you. You keep putting up barriers, and I can't get across to you. You won't let me.'

'Because you're always pretending,' she repeated. 'Come on, Rupert, give. You haven't been honest with me since I got back from my holiday, just putting on an act.'

'You keep unnerving me, and I don't know how to cope, so I fall back on my act—it works with most people. It's only you who sees through it.' He gave her a deprecatory smile. 'It's why I want you back. I can't manage without you.' Uneasily he dropped his eyes down to his plate, and moved some food around warily.

This worked better than he could have planned. Meg believed him. She'd dragged the truth out of him, and he was afraid he'd given away his need of her, so he was frightened. Ashamed too, perhaps. Because Rupert's line had always been that he needed no one. His sudden vulnerability disarmed Meg, and instead of accusing him of wanting her back simply in order to show the world, and most of all St Mark's Hospital, that he could beat Jon Drew any day of the week when it came to holding on to a woman, she softened.

He looked deeply into her eyes again, and she struggled not to drown.

'I miss you so much, sweetie,' he told her, and put a hand across the table.

Meg obediently put hers into it. What else was she to do? And Rupert's hand felt warm and comforting—and so familiar. Now it was Meg who dropped her eyes, as she asked herself what she was letting herself in for. She was giving in to Rupert. Succumbing, as Jon would say, to his wiles. Because he was up to his tricks again, tricks at which he was fantastically skilled. A slick operator, Rupert. In a moment, if she didn't watch it, he'd have her exactly where he wanted her.

CHAPTER TEN

ON THAT same Saturday morning Jon treated himself to one of Long Barn's more lavish breakfasts, and didn't hurry it either, taking time to scan the morning paper between mouthfuls of freshly squeezed orange juice, followed by a meal that even that rat Rupert, he mused, would have passed — crisply grilled bacon with tomatoes and mushrooms. Finally he had a second cup of strong, fragrant coffee, with wholemeal toast and Long Barn's own marmalade.

A grey morning with a hint of rain in the air it might be. Unpromising, you might say. But for Jon the air was spinning with all the promise there could be in life, and had been since the moment he woke. He was having lunch with Meg, they'd spend the afternoon together looking at suitable houses, and after that they were going to have a meal at the fabulous Wheatsheaf.

He was as excited as a boy on his first date, certain beyond any possibility of doubt that he and Meg were destined for one another. He could tell himself to calm down and be reasonable, but his heart knew reason had no place in what was unfolding. His heart was telling him that he loved Meg to distraction, and — and what?

This was where he lost himself, and the glorious certainty evaporated. She was still wrapped up in that useless Rupert. She was coming out of it, he'd seen to that, but it was going to take time. He mustn't hustle her.

It didn't matter. Nothing mattered except that they'd found each other again. She could have all the time she needed. But she was his forever. He knew it.

He went for a brisk, invigorating walk in the drizzle, changed, and drove in to St Mark's, allowing himself masses of time to see everyone he needed to check up on and some over for contingencies. He wasn't going to keep Meg waiting around for lunch.

The morning began well. He just caught the duty physio, who had given Chrissie Mulgrue a work-out. 'I had a hard session with her, and she was very co-operative and tried hard. If you're going to have a word with her you'll find her in the day-room, in a wheelchair.'

'I'll go along there, then, before I leave. You heard about the possibility of a visit home for her tomorrow, I expect?'

'I heard little else—that's what's jerked her into action, no mistake.'

Jon grinned. 'It was meant to. I'm glad it seems to be working.'

'I'll make her first call tomorrow, get her into the wheelchair again when we finish, and then she should be ready for the off,' said the physio.

'Great.'

The ward was busy, and already packed with friends and relatives, as St Mark's had introduced open visiting at weekends. Sister Metcalfe bustled up out of the fray, and took Jon into the office he thought of as Meg's. She gave him coffee, brought him up to date, and then they went into the ward. He examined a number of patients, checked on the progress of others, talked to a couple of anxious relatives and reassured them, then went back to the office to write up prescriptions and sign forms. While doing this he asked about Janey Barton.

'Her mother has still not visited,' Sister Metcalfe told him disapprovingly. 'And she hasn't been to see her husband either, I'm told. A neighbour looked in to see Janey this morning, though, and brought her some nice flowers.'

'Well, I suppose that's something.' Jon signed the last form, pushed back his chair, and stood up.

'The physio's been with her too, and she's got her into the wheelchair with extensions. I'd say she's altogether more cheerful, and much less worried than when I saw her last weekend. A different girl, in fact.'

They'd walked out into the corridor now, and Jon paused. 'Perhaps I'd better have a quick word with her before I go, jolly her along a bit — keep up the good work.'

Sister Metcalfe's mouth quirked. 'I shouldn't put yourself out, sir. She's doing all right, and after all, it is Saturday. I'm sure you've other things to do.' She nodded towards the open doors towards the big bay that formed the first section of the women's ward. 'Take a look.'

Janey, in the wheelchair, was bright-eyed and animated. Sitting by her, and talking away earnestly, was an amazingly handsome young man.

'Mrs Ward's youngest,' Sister explained. 'He's home for the weekend from college, and he's planning, he said, to be here all day with his mum, except he'll go to the canteen for his meals. I was rather wondering if it might not be a good idea if he took Janey with him on one of his trips. Be a nice change for her.'

'As long as you think he'll be able to manage the wheelchair properly?'

'Oh, there's no doubt of that,' said Sister Metcalfe. 'He's used to taking Mrs Ward about in her wheelchair, and he's always very careful.'

'Lay it on, then, Sister. Splendid plan. If it's a success, you might suggest he takes her down to see her father later on. Why not?'

'You're right, sir, that would be even better. I'll keep it in mind.'

Jon smiled. 'Just as Brenda told us, isn't it? Put Janey in the main ward, and half her problems will solve themselves. Anything else before I go?'

'No, I don't think so, thank you. We've covered all the queries I had lined up.'

'Right, then, I'm off. I'll pop in on Chrissie Mulgrue in the day-room, but no need for you to bother. See you in the morning.'

That was what he thought, and at that point time seemed to be on his side. He could have a chat with Chrissie and easily be away by midday. But he was out of luck. He was still talking to an elated Chrissie about her visit home when Sister Metcalfe came in, looking apologetic.

'I'm ever so sorry, Mr Drew, but they're ringing from Casualty. They'd seen your Audi in the car park, I'm afraid, and they asked if you were with us still. I said I'd try and catch you. They've got a patient going into shock. They need to do an IV stat, but so far no one has been able to get into a vein. They're ringing round for a surgical registrar, but so far they've been out of luck; everyone is either tied up in the theatre or at least ten minutes away at home — after all, it is Saturday.'

'On my way,' Jon told her, long before she'd reached the end of her explanation, delivered in fact to his broad-shouldered back as he swung downstairs.

In Casualty he found a controlled air of frenzy among a worried group hustling around a huge, fat, ashen-faced man on the trolley. Jon saw at once that his blood-pressure was descending wildly down into his boots — even though, the way they had the trolley tilted, he was all but standing on his head.

His circulation was collapsing, and, once down, they might never be able to get it up again. He needed instant fluid replacement. Until someone got into a vein, though, nothing could be given. They had already tried more than once, there were black and blue marks on his arms, but, as Sister Metcalfe had said, so far no one had succeeded in finding a vein hidden beneath the layers of fat.

Everyone watched tight-lipped — the tension was palpable — as Jon in his turn began feeling for a vein. If he failed to get into a vein within the space of two or three minutes, they'd lose the patient. Inevitably. The time span was as narrow as that. If he didn't succeed, the fat man would die, there on the trolley in Casualty, as they all stood around him. The trouble was that, covered as he was in layers of fat, finding a vein could so easily be impossible. It was hardly surprising that so far none of them had managed it.

Jon felt around with his fingers, but all there was was fat and more fat. He reminded himself bracingly that at the Midland he'd been renowned for his instinct, his flair, for finding a vein when everyone else had given up. He hoped for the sake of the fat man's future that this flair wasn't going to desert him today.

His consciousness seemed to transfer itself to the tips of his fingers as they skidded around on the patient's sweaty skin. He wiped the area momentarily drier, and felt again. Was there, for a brief second, the faintest indication of a fine ridge somewhere there below the fat? He felt again, found it, lost it, found it, and slapped it to bring it up a bit.

At this sign everyone jerked, and he knew they hadn't dared to believe he'd be able to bring it off. They'd all tried, and knew exactly how impossible it was. They were expecting another failure, and they were hating the ominous approach of failure, the final loss of a life that it had been in their hands to save. Their despondency was thick in the air. Jon pushed the outside world out of his mind, narrowed his consciousness to his fingers and that fine ridge beneath the fat — or had he imagined it? He slapped what he hoped was the vein again, fixed it with his thumb to hold it, and cut down.

He was in. He'd made it!

The tension broke, and teamwork took over, as well as a rushed crescendo of appreciation, relief, and amazed congratulations. Action accelerated. They were only at the beginning of their attempt to save this man's life, and it was another two and a half hours before Jon dared leave the hospital, the fat man established at last in Intensive Care. He'd made a space, much earlier, to ring Meg and cancel their lunch together.

He'd been fed up, of course, and apologetic, but in an odd way the broken date had hardly registered by then. He'd known, from years of experience, as he was tearing downstairs to Casualty, that his lunch engagement had once again gone for a burton. Par for the course. It happened so often. Wouldn't you know, he'd told himself sardonically, that if this has to happen it would be now, when it would put paid to his lunch with Meg, and not an hour earlier or later?

Not for the first, or the last time most of Saturday had disappeared without trace. He didn't really care, though. He didn't, to be honest, care about anything except that soon he'd be meeting Meg.

He arrived at Ferry Cottages promptly, and began to apologise for having had to cancel lunch at such short notice.

'It didn't matter a bit,' Meg assured him. Her eyes shone; she had changed into a favourite evening skirt with a Jacobean pattern of leaves and flowers in a medley of clear colours — scarlet, tangerine, turquoise, cinnamon, apricot. With it she was wearing an apricot silk top with that season's dropped shoulder and full sleeves, and her heavy amber cross, a discovery in one of Halchester's tiny antique shops hidden away up a narrow climbing alley.

'You look magnificent,' Jon told her at once, his eyes roving up and down her slight form in a manner she couldn't possibly mistake.

'So do you,' she responded lightly, allowing her own

eyes to roam as thoroughly, though her simmering excitement escalated furiously.

'Let's agree, shall we, that we make an astonishing and magnificent pair? No doubt we shall be, as they say, the cynosure of all eyes at the Wheatsheaf.'

'Everyone will be stunned,' Meg agreed, though naturally she hadn't the slightest idea that she was speaking the exact truth. She was preoccupied, too, with her own news, longing to blurt it all out, though she succeeded in containing herself until they reached the coffee. Until then they spent the time discussing Chrissie Mulgrue and her visit home the following day, the news about Janey and Mrs Ward's youngest, and then, finally, the house particulars Jon had received from the agents.

'Would you have time to come and view these three with me tomorrow morning?' Jon asked. He fully expected her to say no, sorry, tomorrow was booked. He'd read the brightness of her eyes, sparking unquenchably with hidden yet unmistakable triumph, and his own mood had sagged. She and Rupert had come together again. They'd made up. It was written all over her, and he could hardly bear it. Not only for the obvious reason that Rupert was wrong for her, not only for the inevitable distress that had to lie ahead — Rupert, Jon was sure, was an incorrigible womaniser and would be unfaithful to Meg with appalling regularity, whatever promises he might make.

His own pain, though, was much greater than any of his anguished fears for Meg. He'd lost her. His own Meg, whom he should have snatched years ago instead of chasing, bemused, after that worthless Drusilla.

Young and heedless in those far-off days, he'd been hopelessly taken in, had followed a dream that existed entirely in his own imagination, blind to the pure gold alongside him. Meg herself.

He forked up his delicious cheese and spinach soufflé, demolished perfectly cooked salmon in sorrel sauce with buttery new potatoes and mange-tout peas, and talked with iron determination about room sizes and aspects, easy access, or surveys and potential dry-rot or woodworm. And all the while his heart was quietly breaking.

She sat opposite him, his Meg, her dark hair curling against soft skin still warmed by last summer's sun, a sprinkling of freckles scattered across her small nose. She was wearing a yellowish sort of blouse that hid everything, and yet he desired her more than he'd ever desired anyone, though desire, incredibly, was an unimportant part of the tumult possessing him. The pain of loss was all-consuming.

It was his own fault. He should have grabbed her the instant she came back into his life. He'd been far too complicated and careful. He'd behaved as if she were a patient, imagining he had to allow her time—time to recuperate, to distance herself from Rupert. Time to remake her life, and to begin, he had hoped, to love him.

But Meg wasn't a patient in the wards. She was his forever love. He should have told her so as soon as he set eyes on her again. He'd known it then, at once, if he'd only recognised it. He ought to have seized her and made wild, demanding love to her. Daily. Hourly. Forced her to forget Rupert had ever existed. It surely wasn't beyond his powers? Instead he'd behaved with ludicrous caution, as if she might shatter under his hand. But Meg was not fragile porcelain. And now he'd delayed too long, and lost her.

That look in her eyes signalled joy. She'd remade her life — without him.

Suddenly it was all too much. 'What's happened to you?' he demanded, cutting ruthlessly across her judicious assessment of travelling time to St Mark's from various areas of the countryside outside Halchester. 'Something's up. What is it?'

She laughed happily. 'Oh, I've been dying to tell you,' she said.

Jon's heart sank even further. Below his well-polished shoes, down and down, into the foundations of the ancient old Wheatsheaf, down into bottomless depths. She was going to tell him she and Rupert were getting married — next weekend, very likely.

'I've had the most fantastic day,' she went on, her eyes sparkling at him. 'Would you believe, Rupert turned up?'

He would believe. Oh, yes, he would believe. Hell and damnation!

'It was just before you were due, before you rang.'

He'd known there was someone with her when they'd spoken. He could tell she wasn't alone. But it hadn't occurred to him, not then, that it had been Rupert. And what could he have done about it if he had known? Told them to manage in Casualty without him, left the fat man to die, and driven off furiously to Ferry Cottages to do battle for his love?

No way. The patient had to come first. It had been

his commitment to this that had provoked most of the unending rows with Drusilla, and now here came the same problem again. Even with Meg. She understood, in a way Drusilla would never have done, the demands he faced. But the fact remained, if he had just been there with her, today at lunchtime, as he'd promised, Rupert would have been sent packing. And his own world would not have been a desolation.

'He'd come to ask me out to lunch, you see,' Meg was saying. 'So I said sorry, nothing doing, I was booked.' She chuckled. 'You are so right, you know, about him. No spur like a bit of competition. I'm so grateful to you — I'd never have seen it on my own.'

He was right? This didn't sound wedding bells and happy ever after with Rupert, did it? Could he have got it wrong? Could he possibly have been mistaken? From deep down under the floorboards Jon's heart slid smartly back into its rightful position above his diaphragm. 'What next?' he enquired in a voice as steady as if he'd been on a teaching round, though within him everything was turning somersaults.

'Well, he sort of hung around, you know, and I couldn't get rid of him.'

She couldn't get rid of him? Jon's eyes began to sparkle as brilliantly as Meg's. He'd been wrong — gloriously, totally wrong. Whatever had happened to her today, it had not been the *rapprochement* with Rupert he'd been dreading.

'So I thought I'd better give him a glass of sherry,' she was saying. 'And, do you know, he had the astounding nerve to criticise my sherry glasses? He said now I was in the money, I'd be able to afford some decent ones.' She chuckled, and spread her hands in self-mockery. 'I can't tell you how angry I was, and I more or less jumped down his throat and said I liked the ones I'd got, so there. And at that point you rang. Just as well, or Rupert and I would probably have ended bashing each other. Anyway, when I came off the telephone he was all sweetness and light again, and of course he could tell my lunch date had been cancelled, so he invited me again.' She paused, remembering.

'And then what?' asked Jon.

'Then I said, not very graciously, he'd better stay and eat the lunch that was ready. I didn't expect him to accept, but he did. So there I was, stuck with him.'

'Go on,' he said quietly.

'Actually, I was thinking it might be quite useful, to have a quiet talk with him over lunch at home, out of range of all those eyes on stalks at St Mark's. We'd be able to get back on the old footing, be genuine with each other again.'

'And?'

'And it didn't work. He kept chatting me up as if I were a new girlfriend he was out to impress — I've had the treatment once, and there it was coming round again. He wasn't genuine, and a lot of the time he wasn't even truthful, saying things like how charming the cottage was looking and how marvellous the food was, when I know perfectly well he'd never much liked my cottage — any more than the sherry glasses. Not his style. And he'd always found eating at home — cold meat and salad too, which was all we were having — a dead bore. He used to want to go somewhere "more exciting", as he put it.

'Today, though, charm and admiration positively oozed out of him, and I saw how right you'd been all along. He was out to get me back, and it had very little to do with me; it was simply because he thought you were after me too.'

'So what happened next?' He should have had more confidence in Meg, Jon was thinking. He should have trusted her to recognise a fake when she saw one.

'I told him to stop putting on an act.' She smiled reminiscently.

'What did he have to say to that?' Jon was enjoying himself now. Apparently he was going to hear how Rupert had got his come-uppance. Attagirl!

'He said I kept unnerving him, and this made him fall back on his act. He said I was the only person who did this to him, and that was why he wanted me back. So then I felt rather awful — all the horrible things I'd been thinking about him, you see. So he followed it up. He watched me change, and he followed it up. With impeccable technique.'

Meg shook her head. 'It was a bit disillusioning, I must say. First of all, I could see exactly what I'd fallen for originally, and it was just an act. And then it was saddening too. Because at that point he'd really reached me, I'd been feeling close to him, thinking our friendship at least was genuine. I was thinking, too, that he trusted me with the unflattering truth about himself, and we still meant something to one another. Then back into his act he zoomed, and gave a terrific performance, I have to say. But none of it meant anything. It was just a ploy, to get me back so as to spit in your eye.

'Anyway, he wanted me to go off with him, wouldn't you know, the weekend after next—to Paris. He has a long weekend then, a Friday until Monday at two p.m., and he had it all planned. We'd go to Paris together and stay in this perfect little hotel he knows, on the left bank near the Luxembourg Gardens.'

'So what did you say?' asked Jon.

'I lowered my eyes so that he wouldn't be able to read me, and I said, all struck of a heap, like, "But Rupert, how can you be sure of getting in? It's terribly short notice." So then he said, as I knew he would, "Not to worry, sweetie, I took a bit of a chance and it's booked already." Just as it had to be, for his long weekend. That's one certainty about Rupert—he does like to have everything planned ahead, ready and waiting.'

'What next?' Jon was nearly out of his mind with happiness.

'Well, to tell you the truth, I was beginning to feel quite vicious. I could see it all so clearly, and it turned me right off him, finally and utterly. When it had been my holiday at stake, he'd dumped me without a second thought, and a miserable time I had. How I can have been so idiotic I don't now understand, but truly miserable is what I was. Rupert hadn't cared—he hadn't even thought—what I might be feeling. Or doing. And now it was happening in reverse. He'd booked the Paris hotel, and the chances were high that he'd booked Sally too. But he was ready to dump her this time round, because it suited him to take me instead.'

'There are those who would say so what? Too bad. Let Sally take it on the chin; it's her turn.'

'It seems to have been the united sisterhood—I didn't plan it to be; it just took possession of me', Meg told him. 'This is where it all falls apart, mate, I thought to myself, and I looked him straight in the eye, and I said, as if I really wanted to know, "But what on earth can you tell Sally? How are you going to put her off? What can you say?" And I kept my eyes glued on him, and watched him deflate.'

She smiled, the triumphant gleam back, and grinned conspiratorially. 'It was horrible of me, but extremely satisfying.'

'I'll say! And had he asked for it, or had he? What in fact did he answer?'

'He kind of gobbled a bit, and said, "Um—Sally?" So I said nastily, "Yes, Sally. You know, the girl you're going around with."'

'And then?'

'He said, "Oh, Sally. Well, I suppose—I mean, I don't——" and he went on floundering a bit, until I picked him up and said, "You don't have to go around with just one girl at a time, you mean? Of course not. But, as far as I'm concerned, anyone I go around with I expect to stick to the dates they make, and not drop me for someone else whenever it happens to be convenient—and not drop anyone else for me either. So thank you, but no. I won't go to Paris with you the weekend after next, you can take Sally as arranged, and I do hope you both enjoy it."'

'Oh, well done. I only wish I'd been hiding in a kitchen cupboard listening to all this.'

'Gosh, I wish you had too. Because after that it was a bit flat. He was red in the face, and still floundering. I'd expected him to be frightfully angry, but he didn't seem to be. A bit stunned, I think.'

'Don't suppose he knew what had hit him.'

'You're right, it was a bit like that,' Meg agreed. 'Rather as if he was trying to collect himself, but couldn't quite manage to. So I asked him if he wanted any coffee, hoping he'd say no, and depart, and luckily he did. In a mumble, he muttered that he ought to get back, he'd forgotten there were some telephone calls and — um — things he ought to be seeing to. Then he said thanks for the lunch, very politely, and I said — it was a bit wicked, but I couldn't resist — I said, "Sorry about Paris, but I expect you'll have a super time." And he gobbled some more, I opened the front door, and he went through it. I shut the door behind him, and a minute or two later I heard his tyres screeching the way they do, and then he'd gone. And I dare say I should have felt sorry, but I felt terrific. I still do.' She smiled broadly.

Jon didn't know when he had been so glad. Or so relieved. She was through it. She was over Rupert, and she'd come out with all flags flying, her head high.

'We must have a celebration,' he said.

'Isn't that what we've been doing all evening?'

'A real celebration.' He could have turned cartwheels up and down the Wheatsheaf's crowded dining-room. 'Have a brandy,' he suggested. 'Hardly the topmost towers of Ilium in the celebration stakes, but a marker.'

'Jon,' she protested, 'I've already swallowed nearly all this half-bottle of gorgeously scented hock that you've hardly touched—and it isn't as if I need alcohol to give me a lift. I'm high on triumph, I'm afraid.'

'I want to mark that triumph.' He signalled the waiter, and ordered the brandy.

It came, and Meg pledged him across the table, her eyes still bubbling as they met his.

'I've finished my wine,' he commented. 'So I can't drink to you myself other than in coffee. However——' He reached across the table for her hand, and took it briefly to his lips.

Meg gasped. 'Nobody's ever done that to me before,' she told him honestly. 'I must say, it was lovely.'

'It can be repeated absolutely any time you want.'

'Like now?' She gave him her hand. It seemed the natural, the only possible thing to do.

This time Jon, instead of saluting the back of her hand with the lightest brush of his lips, opened her palm, and imprinted himself a good deal more thoroughly. Then he closed her hand over his kiss, and returned it to her. 'A bit of me to keep with you,' he told her.

Their waiter, who had been on his way to pour more coffee, had halted in mid-journey, and was watching entranced, his expression almost as blissful as Meg's.

She was looking at Jon with her heart in her eyes, though she said only, 'I shall never forget.'

The look, as much as the words, went to Jon's head, and words that he fully intended to hold back came spilling out.

'I can give you more than that to remember me by,' he told her.

Now not only their waiter but the entire dining-room was entranced.

'Please do,' Meg said in a tiny whisper that only Jon caught. 'Any time.'

'Like now?'

'Please.'

'Let's get out of here.' He rose, the waiter dumped the coffee hurriedly and reached instead for the bill, while the dining-room, deeply disappointed, returned to its consumption of the Wheatsheaf's offerings.

In no time at all, it seemed to Meg, they were walking together past the inn's low frontage, making for the car park and the Audi.

Any moment now, Meg was thinking, he's going to say, Your place or mine? And she would say, Mine, very firmly, because if Jon was going to make love to her for the first time—and oh, please, please don't let it be the last!—she wanted it to be at home. He hadn't touched her since they left the dining-room. She'd expected him at least to put his arm around her to walk her to the car, if not kiss her as soon as they were outside the building.

Perhaps she'd been too eager. Could he have gone off the idea? No, it wasn't possible. She was certain he felt exactly as she did.

He was flourishing his car keys. This was ridiculous.

'Jon.' She stood stock-still by the Audi. He stopped, looked down at her, his face unreadable. She turned her face up to his, opened her lips. There was a brief metallic clink as the keys fell to the ground, and then his lips were on hers, demanding, urgent, while two arms of steel held her.

There was only sensation and a brilliant explosion of joy so intense that she was shocked, and clung to Jon with the certainty that at last she was where she had always belonged.

Time had no meaning whatever for either of them. Unfortunately, though, there remained others dominated by the clock, and inside the Audi Jon's phone began to emit its imperious and hated summons.

For a few seconds they ignored it, but then they broke unwillingly apart.

'Hell!' muttered Jon.

'Wouldn't you *know*?' Meg sighed disgustedly. 'And it's bound to be the hospital too.'

'Bound to be.' He squinted at his watch in the light from the street-lamp. 'It's after ten,' he said, astonished. 'I told Duncan to call me from ten on if he needed me—I'll have to answer. And where on earth have those damn keys got to?' He peered angrily into puddles.

CHAPTER ELEVEN

JON was due any moment, and Meg was trying to think about lunch. They were going to view properties this morning, and they needed to be able to come back and grab a hot meal. Omelette — that would be the answer. A cheese omelette. Grate the cheese now. They could have hot rolls with it, and salad. She'd wash the lettuce and make the dressing.

As she washed the lettuce, her spirits soared, as they had been doing since the moment she woke. She was trying to keep her joy within bounds, but it refused to be tethered. She urged herself not to be so silly. All right, she and Jon were about to have an affair. It would be a brilliant, fantastic out-of-this-world sort of happening. Delirious. And she was the luckiest.

But. But this did not, repeat not, mean that she and Jon were going to pass the remainder of their lives locked together in unbreakable marriage, living in the same house, sleeping in the same bed, until in the fullness of time, when they were both somewhere in their nineties, they faded away together into the hereafter. That was fairy-story stuff. People did not live happily for ever after.

She and Jon were going to.

Her body and soul were united in this mad belief. It kept bobbing up and taking possession of her, no matter what cold good sense she tried to apply.

Today was different. Different from any other day in her life. She and Jon were going to agree, to decide, that they were partners forever. That was what she believed. That was what she was certain was going to happen.

She put the lettuce into her wire basket, and went out into the garden to give it a good shake.

The Audi was drawing up at her gate. She waved wildly, ecstatically, and lettuce leaves escaped and lay scattered around her on the grass. Jon was waving back, then he was locking the car, and then, somehow, he was charging up the garden path towards her, his arms wide. Could he have vaulted the Audi? Rubbish. He must have walked — or sprinted, perhaps — round it in a perfectly ordinary manner. He reached her, his arms came round her, and the remainder of the lettuce spun to the ground, though of this Meg was unaware. He picked her up and twirled her round, put her down and kissed her as thoroughly as she'd ever been kissed.

Nothing and no one existed except the two of them. Life was theirs for the taking, forever and a day. A thousand days. A million days. All the days there were.

They seemed to have moved into her sitting-room, how she had no idea, and they were wrapped round one another and kissing as if there were no tomorrow. Nothing had ever felt so right.

At the same moment she felt a wild excitement greater than any she had ever known, yet she was calmer and more secure than she'd ever been. She was here, in Jon's arms, where she belonged. And he was in hers. Nothing could ever go wrong again. Fate could never touch them.

The feel of Jon was a comfort that would never go away. It was impossible, ridiculous, but he felt entirely different from anyone else in the world.

Half-heartedly—after all, it was why he was here, wasn't it? And they couldn't keep all those anxious house owners hanging about all Sunday afternoon, poor souls—Meg drew back from his intense lips and said, 'Jon, stop. We must stop.' She kissed him again, hurriedly, frantically—how could they possibly stop? 'We have to view these houses. We're late already.'

He shook his head briefly, and began kissing her ear, and then the other ear. He paused, said, 'Not today,' and gave her a little quick butterfly kiss on her forehead, followed by a series of glancing, tantalising kisses along her hairline, interspersed with the odd word.

'Not—this morning. Other—things—to do. Much—much—better. Agreed?'

'Oh, *yes*!' she gasped.

'Cancelled—the lot.' He stood back, unexpectedly, and Meg lost her balance. He retrieved her, put his arms round her again, but leant his head and shoulders back so that there was a foot between their eyes. Their eyes clung desperately together.

'We need to talk,' he told her.

'Do we?' she asked uncertainly. It wasn't what she had been expecting.

'At length,' he told her. One of his hands smoothed a dark straying curl back from her forehead, and caressed the line of her cheekbone.

Nothing had ever felt so wonderful. Her entire being surged towards him in love and agony.

'But perhaps not this minute,' he added. 'After all, we have the whole day ahead of us.'

She found herself clenched in the iron grip again.

'The whole day? D-do we?'

'Of course.'

And they certainly used the whole day. In fact, it was mid-afternoon before they ate their omelette. Meg was thankful she'd planned the meal in her head so meticulously—she didn't any longer feel capable of planning anything. Lost in an enchanted trance of joy and contentment, she moved around her little pink and green kitchen in indolent delight, allowing her hands to get on with the job of preparing the meal.

These hands, which Jon had loved and kissed with such loving tenderness—but then there was hardly a millimetre of her achingly desirous body that he had not loved and kissed—these hands now competently put rolls to heat, whisked eggs—thank the lord she'd grated the cheese earlier—while her eyes searched, bewildered, for the lettuce she remembered washing. Not on the sink in its basket. Where on earth——? Oh, she must have put it in the fridge. But it wasn't there. She'd been about to ask Jon to mix the dressing, but what was the use of salad dressing with no salad?

'There should be some lettuce somewhere,' she announced. 'But I can't find it.' She shook her head. 'I must be totally out of my mind.'

'Out of your mind and into your fantastic body, my darling. And what could be better?' Jon kissed her small nose in passing, his hands filled with her pottery. He seemed to be laying the table. That was nice. One less thing to try to think about.

He looked magnificent in striped boxer shorts with his gleaming white shirt open, it suddenly struck her, almost to his navel. As he returned she put her arms round him and kissed him tenderly on his bare midriff.

He drew back fast. 'Hey,' he said, 'stop that, if you want to eat that omelette. If you do that it's back upstairs stat for another gripping session — my self-control doesn't seem to be what it used to be.'

'You are putty in my hands?' Meg raised an eyebrow.

'I certainly hope not. And it does seem improbable. About the most unlikely happening I can currently call to mind, bar none.'

Meg chuckled. 'Far-fetched, I agree. Tell me, do you by any chance see any lettuce sitting about? I didn't take it up to the bedroom with me, did I?'

'I feel I might have noticed if we'd shared the bed with a crowd of lettuce leaves. On the other hand, I might not. I didn't really notice much, apart from you.'

Meg, who was wearing the robe she had purchased especially to go with the pink of her kitchen, suddenly slapped her pink-towelled thigh. 'I know exactly where it must be. In the garden, probably all over the path. I was shaking it out when you arrived.'

She peered out of the window into the mid-afternoon murk of late November. 'Well, it'll have to stay there. I'm not prancing around in the drizzle collecting lettuce leaves, that's for sure. And nor are you,' she added hastily. 'Though it might add a lot to the excitement of Sunday afternoon in Ferry Row, I admit. Do you mind frozen peas instead?'

'There is positively nothing, absolutely nothing whatever, I'd sooner eat than omelette and peas,' Jon assured her, kissing the nape of her neck.

'I like that,' she murmured. 'Do it often, will you?'

'All day and every day. Except perhaps not on ward rounds.'

'How fearfully stuffy of you.'

He nodded. 'That's me — stuffy, rigid, hidebound, conventional. You don't know what you've let yourself in for.'

Meg turned briefly from the blue smoke that was starting to rise from the omelette-pan, gave him a quick kiss, and said, 'Oh, but I do, you know. And I love every moment of it. Of you, I mean. And now I'm going to start the omelette, so if you'd like to brew up some coffee we're all set.'

'Oh, we aren't going to drink coffee. Didn't I tell you we were going to celebrate?'

Meg turned, the bowl of whisked eggs in her hand. 'Yes, you did, but ——'

'Remember when I dashed out to the car some time or other, maybe a few hours ago now?'

'Faintly I do recollect that you were actually absent from my bed for three or four minutes at one point.'

'So. Hey presto!' He opened the fridge door, and removed a bottle. 'Our celebration.'

'Champagne! Wow!'

'You aren't going to say you don't care for champagne with omelette, are you?'

'No way — I adore champagne, and particularly with omelette. Particularly with you, come to that.'

He kissed her again, while they were both wreathed in clouds of blue smoke.

Meg pulled the omelette-pan off the flame.

'Now I'll open this,' Jon told her, 'and you can concentrate on the eggs and the pan. By the way, do you happen to possess any champagne glasses? Not that I'm fussy; we can easily——'

'I do indeed, would you believe? Ready for all eventualities, that's me. Owing to the fact, however, that I'm not actually in the habit of drinking champagne all that often——'

'We shall change all that,' said Jon firmly.

'Super! Owing to the fact that, until now, I've not been in the habit of drinking champagne all that frequently, you'll find them adorning the windowsill in the sitting-room. Clear glass flutes with green twisty stems. They may—er—be a little dusty, so perhaps you should rinse them.'

'They're charming. But, as you say, perhaps a wee bit dusty. I'll see to it, while you get back to your pan and start slaving over that hot stove.'

Soon there were two very satisfying sounds: omelette sizzling in the pan, and a champagne cork popping.

They sat at Meg's round table and toasted one another.

'Here's to us.'

'To us.'

'And many of them.'

'Suppose I were to ask, "Of what?"' Meg enquired, eyes gleaming.

'I'd tell you—in detail. Or maybe show you.'

'I'm not asking. I'm drinking champagne and eating omelette, and I'm entirely satisfied with life as it is. In fact, I've never been more satisfied,' said Meg.

'Thank the lord for that. Don't know what I'd do if you weren't. And I may say, my love, you cook a mean omelette.'

'And you're pretty good at opening champagne.'

'We must continue to hone our skills. All our newly acquired skills, in fact.'

'Let's do that. Oh, Jon, I do love you!' Meg put down her champagne flute and reached across the table for his hand. 'I'm so happy, I can't tell you.'

He kissed the palm of her hand again, and closed her fingers over the kiss. 'Do please try, though.'

So she tried. And what with drinking champagne, drowning in one another's eyes and forgetting to eat, finally pottering about clearing the table and clinging to one another joyously every time they passed, it was mid-evening before they left for Long Barn, where Jon decreed that they were to eat their next meal, 'and have this talk I promised you when I arrived.'

'Oh, yes?' She cast her thoughts back to his arrival this morning, which seemed to be at the far end of a long, long vista of unimagined happiness. 'So you did. Is it important?'

'You could say so,' said Jon.

'Why don't we just talk here and now?'

'Good question. But I want your undivided attention, and in any case you're not going to have to prepare another meal today; it's meant to be your day off. And I'm not going to get it because I'm going to be doing this talking, right?'

'You think we actually need another meal?' Meg asked.

'We've only had one so far, and that was lunch, if it

was a little late in the day. And we need to keep our strength up, don't we?'

'Most emphatically we do.'

'Also they happen to be roasting goose at Long Barn, so I booked us a table for eight-thirty.'

'Goose—how yummy! I'm beginning to take an interest in food again, after all. I'd better go upstairs and put on something more suitable.'

'Perhaps so. Delectable as you are in this cuddly pink thing, wearing it at Long Barn might be misunderstood.'

'You mean understood only too well.'

'Exactly.' His arms came round her again and held her tightly, and once again they lost themselves for an unknown period, until reluctantly Meg disengaged herself and went upstairs to rout about in her cupboard for something Jon hadn't already seen. This plan was interrupted by a shout from below.

She went to the top of the stairs. 'What's that?'

'I said wear that outfit you had on last night. With the yellow blouse. You looked brilliant in it.'

'I did?' He hadn't said; he hadn't uttered a word. Anyway, he liked it, and she'd wear it.

When she came downstairs he was on his portable telephone, and her heart sank. He'd been called away.

He looked up and caught her expression. 'Not to worry,' he assured her. 'I'm only ringing Long Barn to check our table, and I've asked them to order a car for you around midnight to bring you back here. I thought it would be good if we ate a meal together without one of us being on the wagon.'

'What a great idea—I was going to suggest we went

in two cars, so that I could drive myself back, but this is a much better plan.'

'I also told them to open a bottle of their best claret for us — we're continuing our celebration, of course.'

'Just being together is a celebration.' Meg kissed him. 'This is becoming a habit. I don't seem to be able to pass you without doing it.' She did it again.

Eventually, though, they walked out to the Audi, drove into Halchester and out the other side to Long Barn. Here they parked, walked into the restaurant, and were taken to their table. Engrossed in the conversation they had begun in the car, they were blind to the rest of the world.

The rest of the world, needless to say, was not blind to them. Long Barn was a favourite place on Sunday night, and there was a large contingent from St Mark's scattered around. Eyes met knowingly, heads craned, and comments were passed back and forth.

Angus and Jean Henderson were at a table near the door.

'They didn't even see us,' Jean breathed. 'They walked right past us, and never noticed we were here. Now that I call a really good sign. I think it may be on, you know. Meg looks wonderful.'

'Very high colour too.' Angus's clinical eye never missed a trick.

'You think——? Oh, I do hope you're right. Let's pray there's a wedding in the offing. They're made for each other.'

Long Barn, who always looked after their own, of whom Jon was now one, was placing the two of them at a secluded table in an alcove where the room narrowed.

Oblivious of the craning necks and the goggling eyes around them, Jon and Meg consulted the menu, approved the claret, chose a delicious starter of fresh pineapple on a bed of lettuce and *fromage frais*, and agreed to the goose, which they were told had been stuffed with apricots and came with roast potatoes and apple sauce.

The moment they were left alone, they resumed the conversation begun in the Audi, which Meg had found startling.

'Yes, it's a pity,' Jon repeated the remark he'd made as they'd driven into the city streets, 'that we're on take-in next week. We're in the clear tonight, I'm free until nine tomorrow morning, but after that it's anyone's guess. And you'll be in the thick of it just as I'm getting clear.'

'That's right, I'll be receiving the patients just as you're thinking of coffee and a bit of a break. Badly planned, I'm afraid. We should have thought of the snags before getting so involved.'

'Too late now,' he said cheerfully. 'We'll simply have to carry on with these snatched meetings, won't we? But it does make it impossible to organise any lunch-hour trips into Halchester in the coming week, so it may not be possible to go and choose a ring, which seems ridiculous.'

'*What* did you say?'

'Choose a ring. I'd like to get you a really nice one, so we might have to go to London, but I'd think we could try Halchester first, wouldn't you?'

'I dare say we could.'

'What stone would you—what did that odd tone mean?' queried Jon.

'Oh, nothing. Nothing at all,' Meg said airily. 'I dare say you always like to buy females rings when you've been to bed with them, and I feel sure we could find something nice in Halchester in a week or two.'

'Don't be daft, woman. You know perfectly well what I mean, and I'm sorry we may have to postpone——'

'Postpone what? You're going to have to spell it out, because I want to hear it, so there!' She set her chin, and rather undid the effect of this by watching him out of the corner of her eye.

'You know perfectly well we're going to get married. And as I said, I'd like to get you——'

'It's customary to ask, if you can bear to.'

'But surely to God, we both know——'

'Call me an old-fashioned girl——'

'I wasn't about to, and you aren't.'

'Damn you, I want to be proposed to properly!' Meg was shaking with laughter now, and in fact had ceased to care whether he asked her formally or not.

'All right, if that's what you want,' Jon said. 'Here and now. I'll go down on one knee, isn't that the style?'

'You do *not* need to go as far as that,' Meg said hastily. 'Certainly not here. I give in. I accept your non-proposal—with eagerness, if you must know. When shall we get married?'

'Well, as I was saying, we're on take-in from tomorrow, which is going to hold things up.'

'You mean I'm going to have to wait until the week after next? That's a bit much!'

'Unless you want to be married in the operating theatre suite? I've not so far known it happen there, but there's a first time for everything. No? You'd prefer not? Whatever you say. Now, let's work this out step by step. First of all, what stone do you like?'

'Well——' Meg looked at her plate. She knew precisely what stone she'd dreamt of forever, but what if Jon didn't like it, or couldn't afford it? She took a deep breath. 'What I'd truly like is an emerald.' She gazed beseechingly at him, though of this she was unaware. 'It could be quite a small one,' she added quickly.

'I don't see why. Neither of us is overdrawn at the moment, or has funds tied up in a collapsing bank, I take it?'

She shook her head. Was she meant to pay half?

'Then let's look at rings,' said Jon firmly. 'Tomorrow I'll speak to the appropriate Halchester jeweller—the management here will know which one to go to. And I wouldn't be surprised if we're able to have a selection brought to us to choose from—here, or at your place, or at the hospital. Leave it to me.'

Meg had a vision of minions from the jeweller's arriving at Ferry Cottages bearing enormous emeralds on velvet trays. She shook her head. Ridiculous!

A stream of Long Barn minions arrived bearing goose and its trimmings, taking away starter plates, pouring the claret.

As soon as they'd departed, Jon began again. 'What I really wanted to talk about is this question of a house.'

'A house—yes, of course.' Meg hadn't thought of it, but she'd have to leave her darling Ferry Cottage.

It didn't matter. With Jon she'd go anywhere.

'Anywhere,' she said. 'Anywhere at all.'

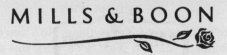

Proudly present to you...

BETTY NEELS' 100TH ROMANCE

Betty has been writing for Mills & Boon Romances for over 20 years. She began once she had retired from her job as a Ward Sister. She is married to a Dutchman and spent many years in Holland. Both her experiences as a nurse and her knowledge and love of Holland feature in many of her novels.

Her latest romance *'AT ODDS WITH LOVE'* is available from August 1993, price £1.80.

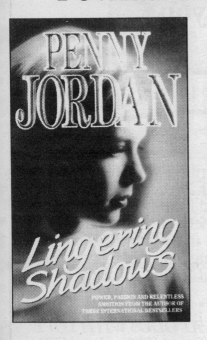

-MEDICAL ❤ ROMANCE-

The books for enjoyment this month are:

JUST WHAT THE DOCTOR ORDERED Caroline Anderson
LABOUR OF LOVE Janet Ferguson
THE FAITHFUL TYPE Elizabeth Harrison
A CERTAIN HUNGER Stella Whitelaw

❤   ❤   ❤   ❤   ❤

Treats in store!

Watch next month for the following absorbing stories:

THE STORM AND THE PASSION Jenny Ashe
SOMEBODY TO LOVE Laura MacDonald
TO DREAM NO MORE Patricia Robertson
VET IN POWER Carol Wood

Available from W.H. Smith, John Menzies, Martins, Forbuoys, most supermarkets and other paperback stockists.

Also available from Mills & Boon Reader Service, Freepost, P.O. Box 236, Thornton Road, Croydon, Surrey. CR9 9EL.

Readers in South Africa - write to:
Book Services International Ltd, P.O. Box 41654, Craighall, Transvaal 2024.